www.dereta.co.yu
e-mail: office@dereta.co.yu

Milorad Pavić

UNIQUE ITEM
delta novel with a hundred endings

translated by Dragana Rajkov

Belgrade
2005
DERETA

UNIQUE ITEM
delta novel with a hundred endings
by
Milorad Pavić

Translated by
Dragana Rajkov

© Milorad Pavić

First English Edition Published
and printed in 2005 by
DERETA
Vladimira Rolovića 30, Belgrade 11030, SCG

Cover painting by: *Tamara De Lempicka*
Illustration by: Dušica Benghiat

Table of Contents:

♦

Chapter One
THE FIFTY DOLLAR SMILE 11
   1. Kenzo 13
   2. Old Spice 19
   3. Poison 23

Chapter Two
THE GOLDEN SNUFF-EGG WITH COCAINE . . 27
   1. Hugo Boss 29
   2. Addict Dior 33
   3. Magnum 41

Chapter Three
THE SEVENTH BULLET 49
   1. Must du Cartier 51
   2. Antracite 57
   3. Envergure pour hommes 67
   4. Addict Dior + Dolce&Gabbana 73
   5. Addict Dior + Dolce&Gabbana + Poison   81

Chapter Four
VERDICTS 87
   APPENDIX
   (THE REPORT ON DREAMS) 91

   1. The first part of the report submitted by Aleksander Klosewitz, at the request of the court
      (The dream of the late Matheus Distelli on the death of Pushkin)
   2. The second part of the report submitted by Aleksander Klosewitz, at the request of the court
      (The dream of the late Marquezine Androsovich Lempytzka)

EPILOGUE OR "BLUE BOOK"
Catalogue of all hundred endings of this novel .. 147

How to read this book:

───────────── ♦ ─────────────

The author has followed the ancient wisdom that says: the ending is the crown and the demise of a work. Therefore this novel is not like other books. It finishes differently for every reader, so each receives his own end to the tale. For this book has one hundred different endings. Like the hundred gold coins that the poor man in a folk tale receives for a magic bird. Thus you can choose whichever ending you prefer. Leave the rest to others. Be satisfied with your own end, you do not need another's.

UNIQUE ITEM

Chapter One
THE FIFTY DOLLAR SMILE

♦

I.

KENZO

Alexander is androgyne. Some pronounce his name as Alex, others as Sandra. Now, Alex Klozewitz (alias Sandra Klozewitz) is sitting in "The Third Cat's" inn and ordering coffee with milk and a bagel from the beautiful black waitress. Alex is wearing a stud in his eyebrow, a blue shirt and jeans. He is sockless, in very shallow black moccasins. His handsome moustache is attached not to his lip but straight to his smile.

"What am I wearing today?" asks the Negro. Her smile has no moustache. Her smile is in verse.

"Augusta, Augusta, I noticed from the doorway that you had changed your attire. Let's see... Of course, today you're wearing a drop of *Amsler* on your wrist. And somewhere else. Not bad. *Jean Luc Amsler!*"

Alex interrupts his guesswork in mid-word, for two well-dressed young men walk in behind his back. Each has a five hundred dollar suit that fits him like it were paid a thousand dollars. Before he notices them in the mirror across from the door, Alex's sense of smell recognizes their scents. One has a sumo wrestler haircut that costs as much as the expensive shoes on his feet: the odour he is wearing is *Kenzo*. The other is black, with a smile worth at least 30 dollars apiece, and has a gold chain instead of a shirt. He smells of a *Calvin Klein* elixir.

Alex instantly shouts out to the waitress: "Another bagel, please!" and flees through the door labelled "Toilet". The two men glance at each other and take a seat, staring at the door all the while. On the other side, Alex swiftly tears off his blue shirt, remaining in a red, female blouse with sewn-in artificial breasts, takes from his bag and dons a black wig, turns the bag inside-out so that it becomes a lacquered female handbag into which he slips the moccasins. His feet are now bare with vividly painted toenails. He removes the affixed moustache and the stud from his eyebrow, reddens his lips and rushes back out. He throws some money onto the bar in mid-stride, yelling in a deep, female alto: "Augusta, honey, keep the change!" and leaps out of the inn with a raised hand hailing a cab...

The two young men watch all this in confusion. Only when Augusta bursts out laughing, in verse once more, do they leap up hastily and run after Alex, who is now Sandra. After a rather brief chase the Negro catches him, takes off his wig and says:

"Don't make any trouble, or you'll get a couple of slaps. A yellow and a black slap. OK? Now listen! There's somebody who wants to see you. You know who and you know why. You'd better be calm."

They take him to a second-hand bookshop. The back room smells of havanas. In that room sits a huge gentleman, toying with a chopper used to remove the tips of cigars before lighting them. He is surrounded by semi-darkness filled with the sparkle of the golden titles on the sides of books lined upon shelves. Everybody calls him "Sir

Winston", and he is well known for always knowing in advance who would be killed when.

"You don't look well, Mr. Klozewitz," he says in a calm voice. With a hand lacking fingernails he takes a cigar from a gleaming, transparent tube labelled "Partagas", cuts off quite a bit of the thick tip, carefully places the tube back on the table and lights up.

"Take a look at yourself, please," he adds, waving his arm towards Alex standing there before him all ruffled, without his wig, his bare feet filthy, and the powder and lipstick smudged across his face.

"Besides, you owe me too much, far too much, and all the agreed repayment dates have long since passed. What is your occupation, exactly?"

"I'm a tradesman," retorts Alex warily, taking the moccasins from his handbag and pulling them on. "Besides," he adds, "your mirror will show what it is that I do." And he steps up to the large looking-glass hanging across the bookcase.

As if on a sign, all faces turn in that direction. There, in the crystal glass, the image of the ruffled Alex is replaced by the reflection of a beautiful, perfectly made-up woman in a white dress. Of the kind that can warm furnaces with her heart. In her bun she wears a wide-spread fan sprinkled with stars from the constellation "Cancer".

After a moment of amazement and doubt the first to gather his senses is the gentleman with the cigar. He wants to laugh, but sneezes instead and says:

"Illusionism, I see. Skillful, very skillful, Mr. Klozewitz. But whatever it is that you trade, you're not doing well. You will never be able to repay me that way. We shall have to make some other arrangement, or else things will not be good. Are you willing?"

Alex nods, and the gentleman with the cigar takes two photographs and a key from a drawer. He hands them to Alex across the table. Then he says:

"So, we are offering you a deal. There are two persons, those on these photographs here, that are an immense hindrance to us. You are to get rid of them. Forever. Here are their addresses and names. By the way, this is the key to the gentleman's private elevator at work. OK? Do we understand each other? Better for you to take care of them then to be taken care of by us, Mr. Klozewitz. And so that there be no confusion, I would like to show you something now."

With those words the man turns towards the Negro and asks:

"Which hand do you shoot with, Asur?"

"The right. I use the left to throw my knife."

"And you, Ishigumi?"

A gorgeous 50 dollar smile spreads across Ishigumi's face. He replies:

"I shoot with my right, boss. And I need not shoot twice. I need not use my left."

"Then stretch out your left hand, we don't want to harm the business."

And as soon as Ishigumi stretches out his left hand, his boss, with a single movement swift as lightening, slices off the top joint of his little finger with the cigar chopper and holds it up in the air, still bloody.

Ishigumi bends over, smelling a bit more strongly of *Kenzo*, stuffs the remainder of his little finger into his mouth and rushes out of the room. His boss now carefully places Ishigumi's finger in the transparent tube labelled "Partagas", corks the tube and hands it to Alex.

"This is a reminder, Mr. Klozewitz. As you can see, there is plenty of room inside for your own two little fingers as well, or some such thing, to be placed there by Mr. Ishigumi if you do not complete this matter of interest to us. Now you may go. I bid you good day."

Alex walks out into the street, blinded by the sunlight, takes a few steps, turns the corner, finally catches a cab, gets in and opens the tube with Ishigumi's little finger. He sniffs the finger with disgust and tosses it out the window, muttering:

"An ordinary rubber finger. And I was supposed to fall for that. As though I had no nose."

2.
OLD SPICE

The photograph portrays a middle-aged man, his face peeking out from an "Armani" shirt as if to say: "People should not think. As soon as you start thinking, you realize you're a dunce." On the back of the picture are the following words:

*Isaiah Cruise, betting-shop manager,
city hippodrome.*

Alex places the photograph and the small key in his pocket, the afore-mentioned shallow moccasins onto his feet, attaches an irresistible moustache to his smile and sets off to the hippodrome. To check out the area. For, he knows that the one with the cigar has gobbled up the joke. And that he would have to obey him. At least for the time being.

The main building has four floors, and the fourth leads straight to the manager's office. Three buttons in the elevator can be freely be punched, but the fourth can only be used with a key. Alex inserts the key into the lock beside the number 4. It fits perfectly, but Alex doesn't wish to turn it, for that would take him upwards and drop him off straight into the office of the man from the photograph. And it is not time for that yet. He puts the key back in his pocket and sets foot out onto the stands.

No race is taking place just then. Several horses are trotting down the track. It smells of the male sweat of studs and the sharp sweat of young mares. Alex turns around, determined to keep searching and to try to spot Mr. Cruise somewhere if he possibly can. In this search he now finds himself on the dog track. Quite a crowd has gathered there. Greyhounds are racing at the moment. They are feverishly chasing after the electric rabbit.

Alex walks between the rows and steps out onto the grass beside the track. He spots a huge regal "Borzoi" underneath a sunshade. The hound is white all over and is standing beside a table alongside which the famous opera singer Matheas Distelli is reclining in a bamboo armchair. Distelli's golden mane glistens in the sunlight like a halo and he looks irresistible, even better than on the stage. On the table in front of him is a golden snuff-egg. The middle-aged lady sitting with him has just eaten a piece of cake. She stretches out the palm of her hand towards the hound, who places his head upon that palm and the middle-aged lady redoes her lips using his eyes for a mirror. Her mouth now looks like a strawberry.

At that moment Alex Klozewitz is washed over by a breeze bearing the smell of snuff mixed with something that resembles cocaine; the strong odor of the hound's fur heavily doused with *Bvlgari* perfume and the name of the middle-aged lady called out by the good-looking man beside her drift along with it:

"Lempytzka! Put on your shoes!"

He has just reached the conclusion that Distelli's voice sounds different in the opera, and that he is perhaps a bit hoarse at the moment, when that same breeze brings Alex the smell of racing greyhounds and the scent of the incredibly old-fashioned after-shave lotion *Old Spice*. Alex turns and, almost in mid-air, catches a glimpse of the man from his photograph. Isaiah Cruise is shorter than might have been presumed. The shirt he is wearing is expensive, but fits him as though it were stolen...

Alex realizes that his efforts for the day have not been fruitless. As he prepares to leave he turns around and glances towards the trio: Matheas, Lempytzka and the Russian hound. The hound is warming his muzzle the length of a champagne bottle between the legs of his master. Lempytzka removes her shoes once more and rubs one foot against the other beneath the table. She is not watching the race at all. Just then she is as blind as time.

3.

POISON

Alex Klozewitz once more encounters the usual struggle with shaving this morning. His mirror image, named Sandra, is causing him difficulties again. Since, like every mirror image, she must imitate his every movement, as soon as he starts to shave his head the beauty in the mirror starts brushing her magnificent navy-blue hair, and as he lathers his face she applies powder to her cheeks. Alex can see nothing in the looking-glass because of her and finally shaves by touch. Then she says:

"And you are really going to go through with this?"

"I have no choice, as you know; our projects are too costly," he replies curtly.

"That does not excuse you. I will have no part in this. It was your decision to incur that debt, not mine."

"What you are saying is ridiculous, considering the fact that we are one and the same androgyne being."

"Which is why you know full well what I can do to you if I decide to put a curse on you."

"You can do nothing, for I have shaven my head. All your curses will slide off me..."

He sprays *Envergure* of the Parisian make "Bourjois" behind his ears and on his wrists before he leaves, and Sandra, copying his movements in the mirror, applies her scent, *Antracite*, to those same spots.

Then Alex puts on his moustache and departs. The picture that he is carrying in his pocket today shows a woman in the prime of life with an irresistible smile. That smile bores dimples in her cheeks and weaves into her dangling earrings. Her name is Livia Hecht, and she works on the 18th floor of the "Plusquam City" bank. She is chairwoman of this institution.

A Mercedes drives her to the front door of the bank, and before she rushes into the lobby of her banking temple, Alex manages to spot several details about her. Lady Livia Hecht's smile always finishes before its end as if it were bitten off; the remainder of that smile lingers on her face like a gutted fish. The lilac eyes of Lady Hecht command the unspoken "follow my gaze" and translate her German face into French, and mixed with her *Poison* perfume she bears a trace of some other scent, one that prevents *Poison* from being fully expressed. Alex has to run and catch another whiff of the trail of scent that remains behind Lady Hecht in the lobby resembling the upside-down hull of a huge ship before he realizes what is in question. Now he knows. The scent of some gentleman mingles with the feminine scent of this Lady. A rather banal one - *Dolce & Gabbana*.

So, on top of her *Poison* perfume Lady Hecht is wearing a masculine scent, *Dolce & Gabbana*. And now he needs to find the owner of this other scent.

Alex Klozewitz spends days searching the lobby and the floors of the "Plusquam City" bank. In one of the queues in front of the cashiers' desks he detects the trail of *Dolce & Gabbana*, but it is worn by some elderly lady who had mistakenly grabbed hold of her husband's bottle instead of her own that morning. *Dolce & Gabbana* engulfs Alex Klozewitz for the second time in the elevator, coming from an old gentleman that squeals like a kid goat with his every breath. Alex finally pops into the safety deposit-box department as well. As he talks to the woman employed there, he discovers, in the next room, a handsome green-eyed man, head of the special department for high-security deposit boxes who has a rubber gaze. Alex is tempted to come on to him, but controls himself in time as soon as he senses that the handsome man, whose name, "Maurice Erlangen", is inscribed on the name-plate at the entrance, uses the odor *Dolce & Gabbana*. It is plainly visible through the glass door that the business premises of Mr. Erlangen are also occupied by his assistant, a mulatto woman with an Egyptian-shaped head that is formed by resting the neck on a metal crescent instead of a pillow at night.

 Just then the telephone rings, and the assistant addresses Mr. Erlangen with the message that he has been called upstairs to Ms. Hecht's floor. She needs to consult with him.

 The green-eyed gentleman leaves his room and walks past Alex hastily. Erlangen is good-looking, with the head of a female marble statue on top of a muscular body. The *Dolce & Gabbana* upon the skin of the man from the name-plate leaves a fabulous odor behind him and almost knocks Alex Klozewitz off his feet. But he can sense something else on top of that smell. For, on top of his masculine one Mr. Erlangen bears a feminine scent as well. Surprised, Alex concludes that it isn't the *Poison* used by Ms. Hecht, who has summoned Mr. Erlangen up to her office for "consultations" and bears his scent on top of her own. The odor on this gentleman, chief counselor for high-security deposit boxes is *Dune*; the perfume of another woman, then.

Alex Klozewitz leaves, rubbing his hands. The composition of scents has produced a mathematically correct result. Ms. Hecht has perfect taste in her choice of lovers. And Mr. Erlangen has more than one mistress. Apart from Lady Hecht and her *Poison* perfume he has another, one that uses *Dune*.

Upon leaving the bank Alex climbs onto the open roof of a street car and takes a seat. He places a hand before his eyes and stares at his little finger. With total concentration, he imagines the pain that the chopping off of that finger would bring. When the imagined pain becomes strong enough, he begins to shift it. He moves the pain from his little finger to his ear, then his knee, transfers it to his left eye, gathers it on the tip of his tongue and finally spits its out forcefully onto the street like a piece of chewing gum.

Then he starts to hum an aria from Mussorgsky's "Boris Godunoff" with relief.

Chapter Two

THE GOLDEN SNUFF-EGG WITH COCAINE

◆

I.

Hugo Boss

Matheas Distelli returns home after his performance, tired and distraught in his concern for his voice that is worn and cracked , though that could not be heard on the stage. But as he reaches the apartment, the hound, entering it with him, starts growling. A sound like thunder starts resounding from the enormous chest of the animal. After that everything happens in very swift succession, like the rapid change of seasons upon the creation of the Earth.

Before the singer has time to do a thing, the hound attacks the stranger fumbling through the room in the semi-darkness. Seeking protection from the beast, that person cries out: "Save me! Save me!", arms cling tight to Distelli's neck and he turns his back to the hound to protect the intruder. There is a beautiful burglar in his arms.

Her blue eyes gaze at him admiringly in gratitude, her arms gently enfolded around Distelli's neck draw him close for a tender kiss, her upper lip hot, the lower one cold, with a sweet tongue between them. That kiss breaths in the singer's *Hugo Boss* perfume like opium. But singers can recognize the tongue of a soprano and that of an alto from the tongues of a baritone or bass. And so, in that passionate kiss Distelli tastes the male tongue of a tenor.

He cuts the kiss short and tears the wig off the burglar's head with one forceful movement. A shaven male head appears.

"Who the devil are you, and what are you doing in my apartment?"

"What do you mean, who am I? One of your fans."

"Anybody could say that. But that doesn't justify burglary."

"This is no burglary. Listen."

And the stranger begins a perfect rendering of the aria that Distelli is singing in the opera this winter. With all the details of Distelli's performance of Mussorgsky. Only, the unknown burglar is a tenor, not a bass. It sounds slightly ridiculous, and Distelli is immune to the skill of the other's singing and it angers him. In the middle of the aria he snatches the stranger's handbag, opens it and from within it he retrieves his golden snuff-egg.

"Not a burglary? Then what is this?"

"I'm a fetishist," the man retorts, "I must have something of yours as a talisman. This is the first thing I laid my hands on. Give me something else, if you won't give me this. Anything of yours. It need not be valuable..."

But the hound keeps on growling, and Distelli walks up to the telephone saying that he will call the police.

"Don't, please. I have something to offer you in return."

"What might that be?"

"A telephone number."

"What would I do with that?"

"That number is worth gold and everybody would love to have it. It is the number of a man that sells the future. He can sell you a few minutes of your tomorrow by transferring it to your today... What could you lose by trying? You will gain nothing from the police anyway, for to them I am small fry, though I'm quite a catch, you must admit."

And with those words the stranger dons the black wig, dictates the number to Distelli so he can enter it into his mobile phone, and then departs.

The number is: 0389-430-23001.

2.

ADDICT DIOR

A wave of *Addict Dior* perfume fills the opera box seats, followed by Madam Marquezine Androsovich Lempytzka herself. She is wearing a "smart" powder that levels the shine of the greasy and non-greasy parts of her face and a dress of the make "Philosophy". The performance has almost begun. The opera "Boris Godunoff" by Mussorgsky is on the repertoire tonight. Madam Lempytzka takes her seat absentmindedly, looks at the programme and starts to read:

    Pushkin's play "Boris Godunoff" was written in 1825, on the basis of historical data by Karamsin and from "The History of Peter the Great" published anonymously in Venice in 1772. The subject is the rule of the Russian Czar Boris Godunoff in the 17th century, who ascended the throne after murdering the young prince Dimitri. The Pretender Grishka Otrepieff dethroned Godunoff, falsely presenting himself as Prince Dimitri, whom God had supposedly saved from his assassins. Ascending to the Russian throne, the Pretender married the Polish Duchess Marina Mniszech Sendomirska.
    Upon examining this play, the Russian Czar Nikolai I, who took upon himself the tutorship over Pushkin's

work after this poet returned from exile, suggested to the author to change this work into prose and posed the question of whether this was a comedy or a tragedy? The poet did not consent to the proposed change and his play was forbidden.

The Russian composer Modest Mussorgsky composed the opera "Boris Godunoff" in 1868, based on Pushkin's play...

Just then the lights grow dim and the prologue at the monastery graveyard begins. Lempytzka nervously awaits the arrival of her lover Distelli on the stage, in the lead role this evening. During the performance she looks on with concern as he uses magic gestures while he sings; he covertly kisses his thumbnail and holds on to a button of his gilded attire. He sings in Italian. Through her skin she can sense how greatly Distelli is envied and how his rivals in the opera hate him. She can tell the different colors of those various hatreds, and the thought that you can no more escape hatred than you can water in your shoe strikes her with horror.

After the performance and several curtain calls for the singers, she notices that Distelli has not appeared before the audience, and goes to see him in his dressing room. It is a richly furnished chamber; there is a bronze statue of him in the role of Falstaff in front of the mirror, a recliner that the hound is stretched out in and a huge cobalt bathroom with a Louis XVI salon in front of the bathtub. Visibly tired, Distelli is lying back in an armchair with a glass of "Chivas Regal" whisky and one of the bubbly wine "Moete" on the table before him. He is still half-attired in the imperial costume of Boris Godunoff, and half into his everyday clothes already.

Madam Lempytzka rushes into the room, the hound leaps up, rises onto his hind legs and kisses her on the lips. He is taller than she is by a whole head. Lempytzka yells:

"Enough, Tamazar, enough!", takes a sip of whisky, sits on Distelli's lap and pours the whisky from her mouth into a kiss.

"You were magnificent," she whispers, "but don't sit there half-dressed like that. The Devil is most wont to attack a man when he catches his at the border."

"What kind of border?" retorts Distelli absent-mindedly.

"Any kind: the border between light and darkness, the border between night and day, with one foot on another's and the other on his own... You look tired. Is singing so difficult?"

"It's not the singing. I dislike that part. Besides, I didn't sleep well last night, and a few evenings ago they tried to ransack my place. My apartment was broken into."

"Did you report it to the authorities?"

"No."

"You didn't? How come?"

"I made a deal."

"In the name of God, how could you make a deal with a burglar?"

"Perhaps he isn't a burglar. Maybe he just wanted to have something of mine. He gave me a phone number in return. It's the number of a man who sells the future."

"And you intend to call this quack?"

"Why do you want to know?"

"Because you look worse than you've done in all the time that I've known you."

"It's the dreams. I've dreamt of Pushkin twice already, in sequels."

"I'd dream of Pushkin myself if I were so involved in Mussorgsky, Boris Godunoff and Pushkin's clowns... Let go of that, relax, and I'll fondle you a bit."

And Lempytzka starts giving Distelli's fingers a "blowjob", one by one. When she finishes with one hand, before she turns to the other she asks:

"And what was your dream? They say that when you tell somebody your dream, its poison passes on to the one it is told to. Speak out! Tell us a part of your dream, and your hound and I will share the poison..."

"I dreamt a room, and by the window there was a small, dark, curly man. As soon as I found myself there I knew that it was Pushkin. And that everybody calls him Alexander Sergeevich. He was watching the blizzard and thinking in Russian."

"But you don't speak Russian."

"Not a word, but in my dream I understood his every thought, and his thoughts were in verse, sonic trochees with a strike at the end of every other line. He kept thinking of demons. How they whirl like snowflakes..."

Just then Madam Lempytzka interrupts him:
"I know those verses by heart:

> *Skyward soar the whirling demons,*
> *Shrouded by the falling snow,*
> *And their plaintive, awful howling*
> *Fills my heart with dread and woe...*"

"Where do you know them from?"

"I know them. Dostoievski inserted them at the beginning of his novel "Demons". And what happened then?"

"At first the dream was cloudy and seemed as though I were looking through water. Then it slowly cleared up and became sharper and sharper. And so I saw that there was another, smaller, pane, a "fortochka", inside the window, and Pushkin opened it. Snow seeped into the room.

"How does one make one of those demons and evil spirits enter the room?" said Pushkin in my dream, "how does one recognize it if it does? How does one make it answer one's questions? What is the Devil in fact? The Devil eats the same as man, but cannot digest a thing. That is because only the Devil does not take part in the global exchange of matter in the Universe. If he has a glass of red "Tokay" wine, instead of urine he will pass red "Tokay" wine once more."

"No!" says Madam Lempytzka, and the hound, thinking she is referring to him, gets down from the ottoman lazily and settles on the rug.

"And you learned all this in your dream?" Madam Lempytzka asks.

"Yes. But the dream ends there, and then it continues on one of the following nights and becomes more and more terrifying."

"Why?" Lempytzka butts is. "What is so terrifying in that?"

"The terrifying thing is that there is a huge white hound with a golden head on the couch beside Pushkin in my dream, and I walk through the dream on tiptoe fearing lest I wake the hound, for if the hound awakes, I know this for certain even in my sleep, he will slaughter somebody... And Pushkin keeps thinking of how to entice the Devil. Horrible!"

"Why do those dreams of Pushkin upset you so? Are they so important?"

"Because he is seeking the Devil to ask him a question that torments me as well: how and when will I meet my end? Perhaps the demon's answer will apply to me as well, and that's the reason that I've been having this dream..."

"But darling, they're just verses."

"What verses?" asks Distelli hoarsely.

"Pushkin wrote a poem, "Laments of a Traveler", in which he poses such questions as when and where, in what ditch his life will end. A quite insignificant poem, and that's why I know it. In Vienna we made friends with the children of Russian emigrants, and Erwin (with whom I was intimate to the waist then) and Dieter (with whom I was intimate from the waist down) translated the poem into German and presented it as the poem of some German poet to Lisa, the daughter of a Russian White Guard, who was a twit. We asked her to translate the verses into Russian and promised that Dieter would publish her translation in the papers. It was quite a comedy. And you, darling, take everything too seriously."

"You think so because you don't know the full story. There is something even more terrible."

"What could that be?"

"The terrible thing is that I bought that dream."

"You buy your own dreams? I don't understand how that can be?"

"I was not meant to dream this dream now. I was to dream it in three weeks' time. But I paid to dream it last night, ahead of time, you see..."

"What are you saying, darling? Here, look at me; eyes are like whisky, there's always a bit of truth at the bottom of them. Let's see... You know what, I believe that you regularly visit this man that sells the future, this quack who sells Friday for Monday. And you conceal this. Admit that you have called the number given to you by the burglar!"

"Well, what of it if I do visit him?"

"If you go, I shall go with you. I want to see what he wants from you. Or is it a woman?"

"No. But I must be alone. It's one of the conditions."

"One of the conditions? So there are more, then. This person is blackmailing you. And he must be asking for money. Don't tell me that he sold you your dream and that you were dumb enough to pay him? We shall go together tomorrow. I want to see him as well."

"We can go together tomorrow, but to the hospital. I have an appointment at the cancer ward. I must have my throat checked out."

"For cancer?" Madam Lempytzka screams and stares at Distelli, horrified. She tries to delve into the secret lurking behind this terrible truth. She knows that secrets have always been older than the truth.

3.

MAGNUM

Dear Lempytzka,

Don't be surprised that I'm writing you an e-mail instead of calling you on the phone, but my voice no longer serves me, so I don't use my mobile. I could send you SMS messages, but, as you know, I don't know how to do that. That's why I left my mobile at home. I'm sending you this letter from the hospital and writing it on the notebook computer that I brought with me, for I'm to stay here for quite a while. I've cancelled all my parts for this opera season, and I had to come here once more last night, for a lengthy period of time. Besides, I never did like the part of Boris Godunoff. My results are not good, but I have somebody who makes things easier for me. It's my "seller of dreams", as you call him. However much you mind my seeing him and speaking with him occasionally, he's taught me how to divide my pain, which is getting harsher and harsher, into smaller slices like rinds of cheese, and digest it bit by bit with greater ease. He knows that illness has a soul of its own. It works on its own behalf within us and battles with our souls. You wish proof of the soul of illness? Here, it is at hand: of all the cells of the human organism, only the cells of cancer are indestructible. Eternal, therefore.

I've been having terrible dreams again at night, I'm dreaming of Pushkin once more. In my dream he's reclining in a 19th century armchair, gazing at the portrait of his great-grandfather from the 18th century. Before him there's some kind of small chest filled with old coins, with several African needles. Pushkin is pensive, but this time his thoughts are not in verse, nor in Russian. Can you imagine, he was thinking in French! I didn't know he could speak French so well in his sleep. Although I understood every word, I grasped nothing of what was going through his head.

"A little African magic of my great-grandfather Hannibal," he was thinking, "and some Balkan magic of Count Ragusinsky won't be amiss..."

Suddenly Pushkin shouted out a name so loudly that he almost woke me up.

"Arina Radionova! Dada!"

An old lady appeared, whom he instructed to bring three rag dolls from the kitchen, and she handed him three finely sewn creatures with wide skirts used as tea cozies or covers for cookie baskets and bowls of hard-boiled eggs, to keep them warm...

That's where the dream breaks off, and it always breaks off in precisely the seventy-first second of dreaming. But I don't regret the awakening, for it's better for my dream to be interrupted by the "seller of the future" than to be interrupted by pain.

That pain is the reason that I am writing you this letter. The pain might become unbearable soon, and in that event I shall need your help! Go to my apartment (you have a key) and take the object wrapped in a purple scarf from the drawer in the bar. And bring it to me. Let's hope it will not be necessary, but I would prefer it close at hand in case I need to do away with my pain. I have arranged with the doctor to be released from here for an hour the day after tomorrow, and we shall meet around 5 p.m. in the coffee-shop "Happiness Begins with T" where we usually have our tea. You will give me the object in the purple scarf, and I will disclose to you the great news that I have been wanting to share with you for the past few days. It is a piece of good news finally, and has to do with my health!

I love you. Check in on Tamazar. He's with that mute Selina.

Your Distelli

Δ

With a kind of sense that time can get stuck and then flow in some direction that it has never flown in before, Madam Marquezine Androsovich Lempytzka goes to Distelli's apartment on the agreed day, pops in to the "mute" Mrs. Selina's in the neighborhood to kiss Tamazar, and then, as into some unfamiliar cave, she steps into the bedroom of the singer where she has spent many an agreeable hour. On the table she finds an open book, "Du bon usage de la lanteur", sits on a small glass barrel that serves as a stool, and at the bottom of the drawer in the bar she finds something that takes her breath away. An expensive "Combat Magnum", and loaded at that. All six bullets are inside it. It is wrapped in a purple scarf.

Her stockings are full of hairs on end, and beneath an enormous black hat filled with hair and fear she walks into the half-empty and dim coffee-shop "Happiness begins with T" that afternoon, orders a cappuccino and glances at her "Chopard" watch, but is somehow unable to read the ciphers on it and does not understand what they are for.

"What on Earth do I do with that?" she asks as she stares at the numbers in surprise, and at that moment she feels the wooden seat of the chair beneath her hand and infallibly senses it to be made of yew-wood. Then she places her hand beside her cup and realizes that she knows the table to be of white maple. At first glance she can tell that the walls are tiled in spruce-wood. The tiles smell of spruce as well... She doesn't have time to be intrigued by her suddenly profound sense of smell, for Distelli enters the room just then. He rushes to embrace he and kisses her first on one, then on the other temple as he whispers in a different, hoarse voice:

"Did you bring it?"

She hands him the bundle in the purple scarf and they sit down.

"Would you like a drink?" she asks him, and he shakes his head no. He is pale, looking at her through triple darkness, but he is handsome, perhaps more so than ever, only his ears are translucent, and his golden hair can be seen through them.

"You haven't been getting enough sleep. Are those dreams tormenting you again?"

He nods.

"Please, don't be hasty with the "Magnum". Even if your results are the worst... But are they?" Madam

Lempytzka interrupts herself, at which Distelli moves quite close to her and whispers:

"I have important news to tell you. I got a piece of the dream I am to dream in three weeks' time from the "seller of the future". And I've dreamt it now. It's also about Pushkin, who receives an answer to the question of how he will die from the demons in that dream, meaning that I know how I'll die as well. Most importantly, my throat will not be the cause! From this illness, that torments me and keeps me in hospital now, I shall recover! For, the forecast brought to me by the dream from my future says that I shall die from the *stomach*, not the throat! And now I must go back. Come and see me at the hospital the day after tomorrow. Perhaps I shall know when I'll be released!"

"I'll take you to the hospital," Madam Lempytzka attempts, but in vain. Distelli drives her to her sister's and leaves her there, continuing on his own.

The stars outside are flaking as Distelli drives to the hippodrome and stops there. Stepping out of the car he feels that the wisdom of autumn can almost be inhaled; for an instant he looks at trees already turned gray, and then, using the key to the special elevator, climbs up to the betting-shop manager's office, the office of Mr. Isaiah Cruise. He finds Mr. Cruise tirelessly going through his accounts and kills him by shooting three bullets from the "Magnum" into his neck. Then he returns the same way that he arrived. When the elevator stops, Distelli takes the special key for the 4th floor from the lock and tosses it onto the floor of the lift. There is no staff at the hippodrome at this time of night, but as he leaves Distelli collides with a brunette in a red blouse and jeans. He departs hastily, and she picks up the key and rides up to the 4th floor.

Distelli is at the hospital once more. He places the revolver containing the three remaining bullets into the safe in his patient's suite goes to bed. As he waits for the dreams to kill the pain inside him, he resembles an undrained glass from which the remaining wine has already evaporated, dried and turned into colored crystal... One regal hound and one perfect crime remain behind him in this world.

When Madam Marquezine Androsovich Lempytzka comes to visit her lover in hospital one of the following mornings, they reluctantly let her in to see him. For a brief moment they are alone. He does not look well, and Madam Lempytzka concludes in amazement that Distelli is saving his glances as though they were money and could be spent.

And then, from somewhere above her, the thought strikes her through her hat: "Glances truly can be spent."

With a final effort, his eyes closed, Distelli hands her the "Magnum wrapped in the purple scarf. She places it into her rucksack hastily, almost joyfully, but immediately realizes that this object is of no further importance in Distelli's life. Or death. Horrified, she calls for the medical staff. They inform her that Distelli has metastases that have attacked his stomach.

Then Distelli opens his eyes for the last time and dies with the words:

"I dreamt that dream again. I was in the future. In that future in four months' time that I shall not live to see. It was irresistible. 71 seconds of eternity... What enlightenment! *At the end of solitude begins death!*"

Already dead, Distelli is frowning as though he had encountered something to be disapproved of at the other side. He makes a few rowing motions with his eyebrows, and quite unexpectedly shifts over in his hospital bed as though he were making room for somebody beside him.

Chapter Three
THE SEVENTH BULLET
─────── ♦ ───────

I.

MUST DE CARTIER POUR HOMME

The man that appeared before Madam Marquezine Androsovich Lempytzka at the homicide department is short, wears a shirt sprinkled with *Must de Cartier* eau de toilette and has one eye faster than the other. Looking at him silently through the shade cast by her heavy hat, Madam Lempytzka concludes: no water is wet to this one.

"Mr. Chief Inspector, I wished to see you because I do not quite understand everything concerning the death of my dear Mr. Distelli, opera singer, who, as you know from the papers, had recently been buried."

"Interesting," lisps the Chief Inspector through a beard of two hues and gestures for the lady to take a seat. She immediately lets it all out:

"I am familiar with the fact that Distelli's apartment was broken into several months before his death, he told me that he made a deal with the burglar under strange circumstances, and that he received the telephone number of some "seller of the future" in return, with whom Distelli met regularly after that. Even his dreams were influenced by this person, whom Distelli told me was not female. Since I have a key to Mr. Distelli's apartment, for I feed his dog, I found Distelli's mobile phone there and inside it the number given to him by the burglar. The number is as follows: 0389-430-23001... Let me conclude. I believe that certain matters could be learned of there, for I do not think that Distelli's death was caused by cancer alone. Matters are far more complicated..."

"But, Madam Lempytzka, the coroner's report is very clear - Mr. Distelli died of cancer of the esophagus, with metastases on his stomach..."

"Dear Mr. Chief Inspector, this is all true, but the secret is always older than the truth. Why do we not visit this "salesman" so that your bewitching eyes can look him over as well?"

The face of the Chief Inspector is lit up by his well-known feminine smile and he rises.

Δ

"Who is in charge in these premises?" asks Chief Inspector Eugene Stross several minutes later into the interphone at the entrance to a red brick building and introduces himself. A door opens, bearing the following sign:

SYMPTOM HOUSE
A. & S. K. - movables agency

Madam Lempytzka and Mr. Stross climb the stairs and suddenly find themselves in a small, pocket-sized protestant-like church with only the most essential ornaments. They are received and seated in the pews of the "temple" by a beautiful woman with large, dreamy eyes that seem to keep falling out of somebody else's dream and into their own. A widespread fan of black lacquer sprinkled with the stars from the constellation "Cancer" is tucked into her hair.

Mr. Stross informs her that he is gathering information about the deceased opera singer Distelli and introduces Madam Lempytzka.

"Are you related to the painter by that last name?"

"No. I am related to the late Mr. Distelli," Lempytzka lies.

"Is this a church?" asks the Chief Inspector. Covertly, whilst the two ladies are engaged in conversation, he takes the opportunity to open the drawer in his pew, and closes it again swiftly. It is nearly empty, except for some transparent, elongated, sparkling object lying at the bottom. The Inspector just manages to catch a glimpse of some kind of inscription that ends in ..."*tagas*".

"No, this isn't a church, this is a trading company."

"So. Good. Would you be so kind as to assist in the matter of certain doubts of ours concerning the late opera singer Mr. Distelli? But I'm rushing things. First tell me, for I'm not quite clear on this, whom do we have the honor of talking to?"

"Sandra. Sandra Klozewitz. Owner of the "Symptom House" company. I'm an astrologer. I'm registered."

"Was the late Distelli a customer of yours?"

"He was."

"What did you sell him?"

"A brief segment of his future, but I do not believe that future can be the cause of death."

"And what did Distelli die of, in your opinion?"

"His diagnosis was cancer."

"You're right, Miss Klozewitz," retorts Stross condescendingly, just when Madam Lempytzka interjects into the conversation:

"What exactly do you trade?"

"I sell dreams. Well kneaded bread and well kneaded dreams are well worth paying for in gold. And they sell well."

"That's just like saying you sell fog."

"What you just said, Mrs. Lempytzka, is a lot truer than you think. There certainly is plenty of fog in dreams, but there are far more dreams in fog."

"How so?"

"The air has always been full of dreams. Dreams are all around us in fact. Not just our human dreams, but the dreams of animals, plants and rocks as well, the dreams of water, which are eternal, for water never forgets a thing, it remembers everything forever. Everything around us is full of dreamed and undreamt dreams. We inhale them during out waking hours, not even noticing them like we don't notice air if it's there, and at night they spend some time inside us nourishing that which our thoughts and our food and drink cannot feed. There's a book in which you can read that all these dreams filling the Earth's atmosphere and the magnetic field above it, all the way up to the Cosmos, form some kind of recognizable shape, or even a huge body, but for us, sellers of dreams, this is of no significance. We are an ancient, though little known, kind of traders. A caste, almost. We are not a religious sect, we're a traders' guild that deals in the selling of dreams, and the dream market in general..."

While Miss Klozewitz is talking, Chief Inspector Stross is silent in such a manner that his thoughts can be heard three meters behind him. Those thoughts are:

"Where do you acquire your goods?"

"In the timeless part of the Universe, where dreamed and undreamt dreams have always drifted together like on a meadow. Each within the appropriate sign of the Zodiac."

"Dreamed and undreamt dreams?" asks Mr. Stross in wonder.

"Yes, precisely. *Dreamed dreams*, for example, have a major role in history, although they don't have the market value they deserve. They drift in their timelessness and are at the disposal of those that know how to cash them in. I'll give you an example:

Let us suppose that, two or three hundred years after the century in which the Greek wise man, Pythagoras, lived, some woman in Punjab dreamed a mathematical operation, a theorem. She was illiterate and didn't understand this dream, and so she forgot it instantly. The dream continued to drift like all the others in the timeless space. A few years before Pythagoras was to come up with his later famous theorem, a seller of dreams accidentally acquired and gave, told, traded or, who knows, sold Pythagoras the dream of the woman (who lived centuries after Pythagoras) and so Pythagoras received "enlightenment" in his sleep, the key to the solution and he "read" and "discovered" his theorem.

"So, to cut the story short, there have been people for ages that can spot and pluck dreams "from trees", so to speak. Then they place them on the market and sell them. I am one of these people. And I pay my taxes regularly. That's all. But I have obligations and kindly let me get back to them now."

As they leave, Chief Inspector Stross appears to Madam Lempytzka to be less crabby, more pleasant (probably due to fatigue after the metaphysical lecture) and distinctly uglier. Taking her leave from him, Madam Lempytzka thinks:

"Dear Lord, he has to pay the same woman a hundred dollars more on each new occasion."

2.

Antracite

At 25 minutes to three on July twenty third, knowing neither the day nor time, a middle-aged lady at the entrance to the red brick building is impatiently pressing the button labeled:

SYMPTOM HOUSE
A. & S. K. - movables agency

As she waits for the door to open, her hat casts a speckled shadow on her eyes and they become multicolored. So beautiful that anybody would buy them, apiece if need be, like eggs at the market. Her breasts are scented. One smells of quinces, the other of pears. The lady likes her breasts to be pinched on the street, but that rarely happens, though everybody would love to do so. Even female passers-by, sometimes. At night she dons a purple nightcap and sleeps beneath a sentence once called out to her in passing: "One like that needs no name!"

"Who is it?" enquires a voice from the black button.
"Marquezine Androsovich Lempytzka."
"You again? Are you bringing the police?"

"No. This time I am alone."

"Well what do you want? This isn't a church, I told you that before..."

"Today I'm coming as a customer."

And Madam Lempytzka climbs up to the "temple" where she finds Miss Sandra, and taking a seat in one of the pews she says:

"What do you actually have to offer me?"

Miss Sandra lowers herself down next to Madam Lempytzka. *Antracite* seeps from her.

"I can sell you a retrospective of your most agreeable or most horrifying dreams from the past century; you will dream them once more at a very moderate price. But why would you do that? You have already seen and dreamed every one of them. I can offer you something better."

"What might that be, Miss Sandra?"

"Our thousand years of experience and multi-millennial market supply and demand have shown that there are few customers like Freud or Jung interested in dreams already dreamt, and that the majority does not in fact desire "second-hand goods" but buys those as yet undreamed, their own or somebody else's, dreams from the future that present a kind of open window to tomorrow, for through them the future can be seen without mages, clairvoyants or doctors.

"Such undreamt dreams of one particular person are the hardest to discern and catch among the countless numbers of other dreams, so they are therefore more expensive. To the person that is to dream them they are of great value, while to other customers they are of hardly any significance at all. But in buying such a dream you're actually purchasing a segment of your future life."

"And how do you know which dream is where among all those that you've mentioned?"

"We know because your dream is a unique item. There is no other dream identical to it. I only need to take something of yours that will help me recognize your dream, like when you give a dog a piece of clothing to sniff so that he can recognize the scent of the person he is to search for. This is a very difficult part of our job. It's like going tiger hunting in order to catch one particular tiger that lives in one particular area, has a name known to all the natives in this area and everybody remembers where and whom he tore apart..."

"You've said so much that I still don't know what you actually have on sale to offer me?"

"Your future. I can sell you a segment of your future. No more than one minute. Or maybe just ten or so seconds more. But you must admit that it would be valuable to receive today a portion of the dream that you are to dream in three years' time, or when you are fifty."

"Is this costly?"

"It is, but not in money. Just as the goods are not in the form of reality. This is not one day from your future, but one night, and a sleep-filled night from your future at that. Let me repeat. The goods are in fact a dream of yours that you are yet to dream, brought into your present."

"What are the terms for arranging a trade with you?"

"There are only three conditions to be fulfilled. Let's start with the easier ones. First, you are to pay me 1000 dollars. Second, you are to open a deposit box in your name at a certain bank. I will give you the card of this bank and the name of the person you are to contact. You must make an appointment by telephone. It makes no difference what you place in the deposit box. It can be but a handkerchief. The important thing is that you get the number of the deposit box opened in your name and bring this number to me, and then I will inform you of the third, most difficult condition."

And Miss Sandra hands Madam Lempytzka a golden-blue business card. She takes it, glances at it and, confused, places it into her parasol that has a tiny pocket on the rim.

As they part, Miss Sandra adds:

"We mustn't forget: you need to tell me your birth sign. I have to know this, for your dreamed and undreamt dreams are drifting in the timeless space of the constellation of your sign; it's a clear day, you'll be able to see where they are tonight."

Lempytzka hands her a card on which there are no numbers or street names, but the stars of the constellation "Aquarius", the sign she was born under:

AQUARIUS

The following day, an employee at the "Plusquam City" bank informs Madam Lempytzka:

"Mr. Erlangen will receive you straight away."

Erlangen stretches out his hand, his rubber gaze on Madam Lempytzka all the while. She is wearing an exotic dress, "Balkanika", created by "Mona" of silken leather, healing stockings "Sanpellegrini" that smell of algae and tea, and a talking watch. Engulfing her with his voice and walk containing a note of *Dolce & Gabbana*, Erlangen leads her to a salon with two armchairs in pink fur, where they take a seat. They are separated by a narrow fountain encased in glass and dark-blue light, resembling a gladiola. Erlangen offers her Cairo coffee that he prepares himself on a hotplate placed alongside the back wall. Then he sits and turns on the music. Mozart fills the room. At the far end of the salon there is a round silver door that leads to the huge safety deposit box chamber. The door is closed.

"What fine activities does Madam Marquezine Androsovich Lempytzka engage in, if I may ask? In her spare time. Please do not take this as an official question. We have no right to that here."

"How shall I put this. Nothing in particular. I loved to read books. But since we have entered the 21st century, or more precisely the Age of "Aquarius", I cannot read 20th century books any more. It seems as though all the heroes from these books have emigrated somewhere and left them deserted. Besides, I cannot seem to grasp what is written for male and what for female readers - And you? Your name, I believe, is Mr. Erlangen."

"Yes, Madam Lempytzka, Maurice Erlangen. I love listening to music here in the afternoon. This is Mozart's opera "Magic Flute"... Do you like music?"

"Oh yes. I like the music of the "Godan Project", and I frequently listen to the CD entitled "The Khazarian Road" or the "Buddha Bar" compilation..."

"Then we are "kindred spirits" in that respect. And what about movies? What kind do you like?"

"I don't quite know. There are too many and I can't choose and find my way among them. I never know how to pick a good one, so I miss out on the best."

"But, dear Madam Lempytzka, movies are easy enough to manage. The past and the future are two blind and mute eternities ahead of and behind us. Since they were invented, movies, sound and video recordings are the only exceptions that preserve that half of eternity behind us. So films must not be missed. You shall come over to my place some time to watch on liquid crystal the best movies ever made. I possess them all. If after the third one you do not admit that this is so, never watch another movie again. But I talk too much and prevent you from listening to Mozart."

Mr. Erlangen rises to pour some more coffee and Madam Lempytzka catches a glimpse of something beneath his jacket that makes her hair stand on end-a "Combat Magnum", the same kind of expensive object that her late lover Matheas Distelli possessed. She clutches her rucksack and asks:

"Does your work not suffer if you spend so much time here with music?"

"To the contrary, Madam Lempytzka, this is an important part of my work. Right now we are actually waiting for our chamber with high-security deposit boxes to open."

"If I understand you correctly, we're waiting for the key to that chamber and this round door?"

"No. This that we are listening to is the key to that door. A specific 14 minutes of Mozart's "Magic Flute" must be listened to and that will decode the lock so we can enter. I change that sonic code every day and choose a new composer. But here we are, it has opened just this instant. Once we enter I shall personally assist you in removing your box from the compartment and then I shall leave you alone with your valuables."

Madam Lempytzka is finally "inside", alone and confused. She glances around the room as though seeking for where an angel has lost its button. Then she starts, and hastily takes the "Combat Magnum" revolver wrapped in the purple scarf belonging to the late Matheas Distelli from her rucksack and places it in the compartment.

Departing with the compartment number in her rucksack, Madam Lempytzka, despite the pain caused by the loss of her beloved singer, the pain that grips her like a tight brassiere, feels some kind of relief, some shameless relaxation now that her lover and the worry for him are gone from this world.

Δ

"What is the third condition?" Lempytzka asks the inevitable question upon her next meeting with Miss Sandra.

"Oral sex."

Lempytzka laughs.

"Why do you think I would accept this? I'm not a lesbian."

"And I'm not a woman," retorts Miss Sandra in an icy tone.

"Not a woman? Well what are you then?" Madam Lempytzka becomes suddenly familiar.

"I am androgyne."

"What would that be?"

"I can be one or the other, but I can tell you that you don't attract me erotically at all."

"No?"

"No. In this case another reason is more important than any erotic plane. It's the only way for me to check if the dream that I intend to sell you is your dream or not."

"Did Distelli have to go through all this as well to get his dream?"

"But no!" laughs Miss Sandra, "his verification had to be entirely different. I don't invent these verifications, they are imposed by the dream in question."

"If I accept, what would this oral sex be like? I have no idea what you actually have between your legs."

"Read Jung, it's written plainly that androgyne beings are not to be confused with hermaphrodites. Bet let's not go into science. You shall come to dinner here tomorrow night. And everything will take place then, at the table. How it will take place depends on you. If you do not come, no harm done. Your dream will remain hanging on some branch or star and will still be waiting for you in one of your tomorrows. Don't forget: I'm not coaxing you into anything. You came of your own accord and you make your own decision... But, if you do come again and this matter does take place, you will dream an insert from your future the following day, or more precisely you will dream now the dream you are to have in a few months' time."

3.

Envergure pour Homme

At the other end of the room, right by the wall, there is a tall cupboard designed to the "Bidermeier" taste of the 19th century German middle class; it has seven drawers and is usually called "Seven Days" since it has a drawer for every day of the week. In front of it there is a laid table and on it dinner for one. There is only one chair in the room. When Madam Marquezine Androsovich Lempytzka enters the room Miss Sandra is already sitting on that chair, engrossed in her meal. The menu consists of sushi with ginger, a sea-algae salad and green tea. A gleam from the green tea is quivering on the ceiling.

    Miss Sandra does not interrupt her meal, though she stares at her guest without blinking. Her hair is shining, her fingers gently resting on the ivory chopsticks she is using to take morsels of rice. But those fingers are encased in gloves. And not just any ordinary gloves. One glove has seven fingers, the other five. Judging by those gloves, Miss Sandra has a dozen fingers. Just as many as there are months in a year. One finger for each month.

    She offers no greeting, makes no gesture to indicate what her guest should do. Lempytzka waits for a while, shifting from foot to foot, and then swiftly throws her hat with the speckled shade into a corner of the room, and kicks of first one and then the other crystal-heeled "Swarovsky" shoe. She recalls Distelli's words:

"Marquezine, put on your shoes!"

Her eyes flow at full speed, her glass mini skirt will not get in the way, and she crouches down on all fours and crawls under the table. She is stunned by two things there: the perfume is no longer the *Antracite* that she smelled on Miss Sandra the very first day, but is now *Envergure*, a gentleman's scent. The other thing that almost shocks her senseless is the male member over 7 inches long that she finds between Miss Sandra's legs. Then Sandra stops sipping her tea and lights a cigarillo with her seven-fingered glove. She holds it between September and October. And so they blow in unison. Miss Sandra blows smoke above the table, and Madam Lempytzka down there, under the table...

When the stance comes to an end, Madam Lempytzka straightens up and looks in amazement at the beautiful female face of Miss Sandra, who says:

"You shall have a dream tomorrow night, one that you were to dream in seven months' time, sometime in March next year. You won't recognize it at first. It will seem like any other. But don't worry. You'll be convinced when you dream the rest of it next year, for I, as we have established, can provide only a very brief part of that dream from the future now. I'll give you a piece of advice. When you dream dreams from the future, you shouldn't sleep in the bed you usually spend the night in. Sleep somewhere else. And don't turn your head in the same direction as you would in your own bed."

Δ

Madam Lempytzka buys her "dream from the future" a gondola the following day. A real Venetian floating vessel in black lacquer. The salesman hangs it from chains attached to her bedroom ceiling, and Lempytzka tosses pillows of various colors into it. In the evening she takes a bubble-bath, puts on a new nightgown, applies her *Addict Dior* perfume that somehow smells of watermelons to her, which she is not too happy about, and climbs into her "floating" nest. Everything that she has ever been told about dreams amounts to a single thought, and she keeps repeating this sentence as she falls asleep:

"In your dreams you should not be deaf. You should remember what is said there..."

The moment she fell asleep, Madam Lempytzka turned into a boy. The boy lived in the large house belonging to his parents. He slept on the first floor in a room located inside another, larger chamber - the dining-room. This was a room within a room, then. It had two windows with pretty curtains through which the family and guests could be seen entering the dining-room, and his mother could peek in at night to see if the boy had fallen asleep.

But sometimes the boy didn't sleep. He would close his eyes and listen. It was always the same. On the windowless wall there was a huge cupboard. Like a third room within a room. And footsteps could sometimes be heard from that direction. Somebody was walking in the nursery cupboard. This didn't occur each time. But it could be heard plainly... At times those footsteps behind the double doors of the wooden giant were close together and restless, and once they walked away slowly only to break into a trot somewhere in the distance. That scared the boy and he sat up in bed...

Madam Lempytzka's dream breaks off just then and, disappointed, she goes to see the "seller of the future" in the morning to find out the meaning of it all. Miss Sandra is not in the "temple" of the "Symptom House". Lempytzka finds a young gentleman there instead, with a clean-shaven head, a moustache, black lacquered moccasins, a blue shirt and jeans. He smells of *Envergure* and is toying with the golden snuff-egg belonging to the late Matheas Distelli. He is wearing a stud in his eyebrow. Lempytzka vents her rage straight from the doorway:

"So you are Miss Sandra. How do I know that you did not trick me? The sequence of the dream was very brief and unrelated!"

"Of course; it is precisely seventy one seconds of your future. It is in fact the beginning of a dream that you will have in seven months' time, next year in March. You will dream the rest of it then."

Madam Lempytzka is so upset that she doesn't notice that the "seller of dreams" is behaving as though they meet for the first time, as though he was never the beautiful Miss Sandra with her knees spread beneath the table and as though they were not on a first-name basis just a few days ago.

"What does this dream mean?"

"Don't ask me that. Experts would tell you that you can explain it all through associations leading up to the dream (Jung), or those leading from the dream (Freud)...

But let me make this clear: I'm not a psychiatrist, I treat nobody, yourself included, I don't interpret dreams, I merely sell them. If you want the sequel to this dream from the future that you purchased, that will be a new order. In that case you must pay for another seventy one seconds of your future, and the procedure will be the same once more."

"I have no intention of continuing. You have abused me. I shall turn the matter over to my attorney. Who are you in fact? You sell so-called dreams by the meter. That golden snuff-egg is the one that you stole from the opera singer Distelli when you broke into his apartment!"

At Madam Lempytzka's words Alex Klozewitz, alias Sandra, begins to hum Mussorgsky, opens the egg and uses the contents to powder his nose. Distelli's golden snuff-egg with cocaine now serves Alex Klozewitz as a powder compact.

4.

Addict Dior + Dolce & Gabbana

Marquezine Androsovich Lempytzka takes her "anti-ageing" caviar treatment and applies "smart polish" to her fingernails, which changes color with every drop or rise in her temperature. Thus furnished she leaves for Cairo with her new lover, Mr. Maurice Erlangen. When they land, her purple nails take on the color of white roses, and Mr. Erlangen checks her into the "Mena House Hotel". As soon as they open the terrace door, Cheops's huge pyramid almost touches their bed. The pyramid is here, within reach, the color of red sand. The smell of it mingles with the odors of their bodies, her *Addict Dior* perfume mixes with the male *Dolce & Gabbana*.

"How old is that monster peeking under our bedspread?" Lempytzka asks.

"The pyramid is skinned, actually, and we can see only it's flesh. It didn't look like that a million nights after it was born. Nor did it have that color ten million nights later. And then several hundred million nights washed over it, and after several such bouts of ageing it began to take on its present appearance and color. And so it turns old and gray."

"You're scaring me," says Madam Lempytzka. Mr. Erlangen comforts her with an embrace and promises to take her to the old Cairo suque, where they drink baked Arabian tea.

Erlangen is an irresistible seducer and they kiss passionately among the Bedouins with camels whose gazes shed upon them. In the evening he slaps her breasts, licks her spine, and during the day she finally has somebody to pinch her breasts in the street, among the goats and vendors of Egyptian bread. In the Copt part of the city Mr. Erlangen is handed a nargileh, and he smokes the aromatic tobacco "Two Apples" through water, while an old lady decorates Lempytzka's eyes in the fashion of the Ancient Egyptians: Lempytzka now has the sight of the Egyptian god Ra, and eyes from 1350 B.C. Her eyes are now the eastern and western regions of her soul... Her right eye represents the Sun, and the eyebrow and border around the eye are black, while the eyelid is pale green. Her left eye represents the Moon, and the eyebrow and border around the eye are dark blue, while the eyelid is deep yellow, the color of sand. That eye is the eye of nighttime light...

When the work is done the old woman says:

"Now listen, my child, to what old Zoida will tell you. You have red pupils like a Goddess. Ask your man to buy you a red stone for your bellybutton. That is what goddesses wear."

Erlangen is delighted and buys a ruby at the first jeweler's, which Lempytzka places in her bellybutton. He takes her in the most incredible places, in public. In a cab, in the elevator, half-dead with fright in one of the small pyramids, in the male restroom of the Egyptian museum, at the old Cairo cemetery inhabited by the living...

At breakfast Lempytzka tells her lover:

"We're both better-looking in Africa than in Europe!"

"Don't trust the mirrors," he retorts, "Arabian mirrors are set to make you look slimmer than you are."

"That's not true. The flowers I recognize from Europe are huge here, taller than I am, and their scent is three times stronger. In Egypt the people and donkeys and goats are exposed to the benefits of phytotherapy and medicinal vapors. It's March in the shade and July in the sun here."

In the old suque they barely manage to find a spot in the small street crowded with tables and chairs on which people from all four corners of the world sit, laughing in a hundred languages at the same time and drinking tea. One Belgian climbs onto a table and infallibly pours tea from the pot into his glass cup placed on the sidewalk from the height of over two meters. Marquezine and Erlangen applaud him, he takes his glass and sits on the pavement at their feet. He introduces himself as Wym Van de Koebus and asks:

"Have you heard the tale of grass? If you haven't, I shall tell it to you. You mustn't leave Cairo without hearing it!"

Lempytzka drinks baked tea while sitting in Erlangen's lap, dozing and, with Erlangen's finger inside her, listening to the Belgian's whispers...

Cairo breaths around Lempytzka and Erlangen, expanding and contracting its huge chest, gaining two million inhabitants each night and losing as many every morning. Lempytzka's shaded eyes cannot tell North from South, nor what's left and what right. March is a beautiful time of year in that region, but Madam Lempytzka neither knows the date, nor does she look at her watch. Until she has a dream one night, there, in Cairo. Actually it isn't a dream. It's the sequel to one dream well remembered.

The Cairo Dream of Madam Lempytzka

As soon as she sinks into sleep Madam Lempytzka turns into a boy sitting in his room, listening to the mysterious footsteps in the cupboard. In a nutshell, even in her sleep she recognizes that she has had this dream before and that it is occurring once again. But at the moment when the boy wants to wake up in fear, the dream continues!

In this continued dream the boy is sitting at the table, the cupboard from which he can sometimes hear the trickle of water is behind his back, and into the room steps Oharaska, his cousin. She is 14, he about half her age, but he does not know how old they are. It is afternoon, time flows with occasional pauses, like it does at railway stations. In the house of the boy's parents everybody is enjoying this period of rest after their meal, and Oharaska is carrying a tray with a glass of raspberry juice and a bowl of porridge. She makes it herself and before she places the glass and the bowl in front of the boy her mouth spreads into a broad smile full of teeth and tongue.

The boy understands the meaning of that smile full well and shouts out, horrified:

"No! No! No!" but does not move from the chair, as though he were bewitched. At that moment

Lempytzka, dreaming that she is a boy, has her first erection. Then Oharaska orders:
"Eat!"
The frightened boy shoves a spoonful of porridge into his mouth and immediately starts drinking his juice, and Oharaska crawls under the table, spreads his knees with her head, unbuckles him and takes him into her mouth, sucking him like a sweet. He stops drinking his drink, and she begins to drink the drink she has just received...

When something thick and sweet is to flow from the boy, the dream ceases and Madam Lempytzka awakens with a cry.

The impression caused by this dream is such that Lempytzka shakes the sleeping Erlangen and says:
"I must return to Europe immediately."
He looks at her with his rubber gaze and laughs wordlessly. Finally he kisses her and says:
"My beauty, we're returning tomorrow anyway. My vacation is over and I must get to the bank..."

Δ

Morning is slightly blind, and spring became none the wiser the day that Madam Lempytzka, for who knows which time, presses the black button labeled:

SYMPTOM HOUSE
A. & S. K. - *movables agency*

"Fuck... you were right! Who are you, anyway?" shouts Lempytzka from the doorway, and without hesitation asks the "seller of dreams" for the next segment of her future life.

Alex Klozewitz's moustache curls into a smile and he spreads his arms:

"Since you have seen the dream, you realize that I don't have to deceive anybody, and I didn't deceive you either. If you had approached the table with food in some other manner that evening, from the other side of the table for example, I would have known that it wasn't your dream. But let me tell you straight away, if we are to conclude another agreement, the matter that I have to offer this time will be more costly."

"What would this that I am to receive be, and why is it more costly?"

"You would receive a piece of eternity this time. That's why it is more expensive, and it contains a certain element of danger. But it would be better if you did not enter into this, for it's a hornets' nest and I'm not sure you'd like what I have to inform you of concerning this, if we were to continue with the agreement.

"You can tell me. I am cowardly, but only about little things. What do you have in store for me?"

"It's a dream you would have at the age of 37. In two years' time, then. Precisely seventy one seconds of your future, one that you shall never have."

"How is this different from the previous dream?"

"I could promise you a dream that you are to have at any time in your life. But this dream isn't like that. This is a dream that you shall never have, for you will not live to be 37. It's a dream from eternity. From beyond the grave. But it's your dream. I'm sorry to have to tell you this, but without that information we could go no further with the purchasing procedure."

"How do you know that I won't live to be 37?"

"Dear Madam Lempytzka, I can calculate these things. If I know the day that I am to die, why would I not know the same about you? You shall not live to see your 37th year. From that year you can receive from me only a morsel of the dream that you would have then if you were alive."

"Can that be done and how?"

"When you catch a bird, you never catch half of it, or a quarter, but the whole bird regardless of whether it is large or small. It's the same with dreams. I can catch either your entire dream or nothing, whether the dream is long or short. Therefore, that part of your dream, the rest of it that you will never dream, drifts in the timelessness, just like birds in flight already have legs and tails, for example. Or I could give you another example. Just as hair and nails continue to grow after death, dreams continue posthumously as well though they were not completed during one's lifetime."

"Did Distelli receive a hint as to how he was to die in his dream? In other words, could I see the undreamt part of Distelli's dream that you caught for him, but did not sell him for he died before the dream's end?"

"That cannot be done. First of all because he received the entire dream and dreamed it to the end. The posthumous part as well. Besides, the terms of sale were completely different for him. All that I can tell you is that your dream, the one I managed to catch, is about a hundred years younger than that of your late lover, Mr. Distelli. His is from the beginning of the 19th, and yours takes place at the beginning of the 20th century.

"What does this mean?"

"For the meaning of it you would have to consult one of Freud's followers, not me. I am not a doctor to heal, nor a mage; I do not predict the future. Nor am I a politician to promise you a better life, or a representative of cyber capital to protect the tomorrow of the great from the tomorrow of the small. I am a salesman and I sell you your future just as it is to be..."

5.

Addict Dior + Dolce & Gabbana + Poison

Madam Lempytzka is sitting in the "temple" called the "Symptom House", listening to what the "seller of the future" is telling her about Distelli's dreams and her own, and she says pensively:

"So you can tell the dreams of your customers apart, like those women that can tell a flea bite from that of a mosquito..."

"If you mean to say that dreams can bite, you're correct."

"But let's get back to our agreement concerning the purchase of the future from beyond the grave. Under what terms could I buy another seventy one seconds of the future that I will never live to see? How much is your spoonful of eternity? You say the conditions are more difficult. Do such dreams from beyond the grave bite?"

"They do more than that."

"What does that mean?" asks Madam Lempytzka. Her transparent tongue is protruding from between her lips as it always does when she is expecting some important reply. She is silent, her eyes closed.

"You will have to kill somebody."

Lempytzka opens her eyes and asks:

"That's one of the conditions?"

"Yes. But, since you won't live to be 37, it isn't something that need overly concern you. For, bear in mind, I don't know when you will die, but I do know that it will be before the year I have mentioned."

"So it could happen sooner. How much sooner?"

"I don't know the answer to that. I was unable to calculate it."

"You are a polite and very well-mannered piece of shit."

"Don't get angry, Madam Lempytzka, but think things over carefully first. Don't rush your decision. If you have any doubts despite your positive experience in dealing with us so far, think what you're being offered this time. If you receive but the tiniest morsel of that future that you will not take part in, a spoonful of the future after your death, a fragment of time after your life ends, then that is truly a great thing to receive. Is it not worth trying and sacrificing something for such a unique item?"

"But whom am I to... if I do make up my mind..."

"Make your own choice. But, dear Madam Lempytzka, it isn't hard to guess whom a person would like removed before their death, when die they must. Is there anybody you hate, anybody you are, for example, jealous of?"

"I don't know. I'm not acquainted with that person. I just sense that such a person exists."

"Well then, check it out and if you find proof, do it. And bear in mind that you have to ensure my presence during the deed. I must make sure that you killed this person. That's part of the deal."

Lempytzka is thinking of something completely different while she's listening. She is whispering to herself:

"I hate my pussy!". Since they returned from Egypt, Lempytzka spoke with Erlangen twice, but has had no success in reaching him on his mobile phone or at the bank. He is always "submitting a report" or at a "board counseling". His mobile phone is switched off when he's at home.

"Does he have a pillow of his own at all? How many pillows does that man sleep on?" she wonders about Erlangen as she leaves the temple where the future is sold and goes to the "Plusquam City" bank in fury.

"Mr. Erlangen is not in the building at the moment, and he has a board meeting later on."

Lempytzka realizes that any further attempt to have Erlangen's secretary arrange a meeting with him for her would be futile and asks for her deposit box to be opened.

In the salon with pink fur armchairs she sits with an employee, some groomed mulatto woman, listening to Bella Bartock. Fury bubbles inside of Lempytzka with every beat of the unbearable music. As soon as the round silver door lets her pass through to the valuables, she takes the "Magnum" from her high-security compartment and places it in her rucksack, leaving the scarf in the box. Lempytzka departs from the bank hastily, almost running. She phones her "seller of the future" in mid-stride and invites him to join her at the villa with a garden and lake where Erlangen lives.

Lempytzka and Klozewitz pause at the entrance to the villa. It is autumn. Leaf towards leaf, an entire grove falls into the lake. The entrance is locked. Lempytzka doesn't have a key to the villa, so Klozewitz cautiously breaks in using his steel calling card. At first it seems as if the place is empty, but a female voice is soon heard from upstairs. The unknown woman, assuming that her host has returned, calls from the bedroom:

"Darling, here I am!"

Then she steps out onto the stairs half-nude, wearing boots up to her pussy.

Alex Klozewitz barely has time to realize that his expectations have been fulfilled, barely manages to recognize the *Poison* perfume and the representative of the "Plusquam City" bank executive board, Livia Hecht, there on the stairs, when Lempytzka kills her by firing three shots from the "Magnum". As she shoots there are three glass tears of jealousy and rage in her eyes.

Just then Alex Klozewitz smells *Dolce & Gabbana* fill the house, quickly ducks behind one of the curtains by the front door, and Erlangen enters the hall. He heard the shots on his way home from work, saw the front door forced and took out his "Magnum".

He yells:

"Lempytzka, drop the weapon!" but Lempytzka turns her "Magnum" towards him in rage and they both fire at the same time. Madam Marquezine Androsovich Lempytzka falls dead on the spot, while Erlangen is not so much as grazed. Lempytzka's revolver was empty - in it there was no seventh bullet.

Alex Klozewitz now has to figure out how to sneak out of the house unnoticed, although he is but two paces away from Erlangen. Erlangen coolly takes his "Sony Ericsson" mobile phone and calls the police. Just then Klozewitz notices that the "smart polish" on Madam Lempytzka's blue nails is turning peach, then yellow, green and red, and the tears of jealousy and rage on her cheeks into broken glass. He wonders: which is the color of death? leaves his shelter and approaches Erlangen from behind with the words:

"What in the world is going on here?"

"Who the hell are you?" asks the master of the house.

"A passer-by. I heard shots, saw the open door and came in to see if you needed help. And now I'm your witness and your alibi. I'll testify that you fired in self-defense. But I must go now. I'll leave you my telephone number. Feel free to call me. My name is Erwin."

And Klozewitz gives the number 0389-430-23066 for Mr. Erlangen to enter it into his mobile and leaves hastily as the wail of police sirens is heard in the distance.

Chapter Four
THE VERDICTS

♦

During the trial of Maurice Erlangen for the murder of Madam Marquezine Androsovich Lempytzka, the attorney of her sister, Sophia Androsovich, and the representative of the late opera singer Matheas Distelli raised another charge: against Alexander Klozewitz and his trading company "Symptom House", for profit gained in an illegal manner by trading dreams to Distelli and Lempytzka.

The Court has reached verdicts in two separate proceedings:

- Maurice Erlangen is sentenced to jail for exceeding measures of necessary self-defense at the time of the murder of Lempytzka.
- The Court has established illegal gain of profit in the business operations of A. Klozewitz, for his customer, the late Madam Lempytzka, did not receive the agreed good despite fulfilling all obligations towards the seller. This verdict is based on the confession of the accused, Alexander Klozewitz himself, which is as follows:

"Although Madam Marquezine Lempytzka fulfilled her obligations towards "Symptom House" in a timely

fashion, the posthumous part of her dream could not be delivered in advance, for Marquezine was murdered before the delivery was able to reach her. I am prepared to reimburse her inheritors for the profit, if we assume the said profit to be gained in an illegal manner, although I do not see myself at fault in this matter, considering the occurrence of "vis major".

On the basis of this confession, the Court has ordered Alexander Klozewitz to reimburse the inheritor of the late Marquezine Androsovich Lempytzka, Miss Sophia Androsovich, for the damage caused by the fact that Klozewitz did not deliver the goods paid for, and thus gained profit in an illegal manner.

- Alexander Klozewitz is found not guilty of the charge of failing to deliver the agreed goods (71 seconds of the posthumous future of Mr. Distelli), for the goods were delivered in full, which can be concluded on the basis of two facts:

A. This matter is confirmed by the statements of the doctors, who heard (as did Lempytzka, who was also present) Distelli say in agony that he had been to the future, and add: "At the end of solitude begins death." This, as we can see from the reports on the dreams submitted to this Court by Klozewitz, is the final sentence in Distelli's dream.

B. Due to the fact noted in item A. of this verdict, Madam Lempytzka then concluded an agreement of her own with Klozewitz, for she had verified that Distelli, her lover, had not been deceived in the matter of his purchasing agreement.

In short, Klozewitz delivered the entire dream to Distelli; therefore, Distelli dreamt the dream about

Pushkin to the end, and the salesman cannot be charged for the gain of profit in an illegal manner in this matter, since he delivered the agreed "movables", as he puts it, in full.

- Finally, it should be noted that the court could not establish a connection between the Lempytzka case and the murder of the hippodrome betting-shop manager Isaiah Cruise, which murder remains unresolved at this time despite the efforts of Chief Inspector Eugene Stross, who is in charge of this case as well.

Note

During the proceedings of the Distelli-Lempytzka case, the "Symptom House" company was ordered to submit certain information to this Court. This information consists of reports on the dreams sold to Distelli and Lempytzka by the "Symptom House". These reports were filled out and signed by Alexander Klozewitz and they are filed separately in the court documentation on the Distelli-Lempytzka case. During the investigation Chief Inspector Stross discovered that "Symptom House" is also in the possession of two tapes containing descriptions of the dreams sold to Distelli and Lempytzka. Both dreams are described on tape in the voice of Klozewitz.

The report submitted by Klozewitz to this Court and the text of the tapes are laid out in the *Appendix* herein.

APPENDIX

REPORT ON THE DREAMS CONTAINING:

---------- ♦ ----------

1. "The dream of Pushkin's death", which was the subject of the purchasing agreement between the opera singer Mr. Matheas Distelli as buyer and the "Symptom House" company as seller.

2. "The dream of footsteps", which was the subject of the purchasing agreement between Madam Marquezine Androsovich Lempytzka as buyer and the "Symptom House" company as seller.

THE FIRST PART OF THE REPORT SUBMITTED BY ALEXANDER KLOZEWITZ AT THE REQUEST OF THE COURT

(TAPE 1)

"*For the needs of the court investigators and Chief Inspector Eugene Stross I, the undersigned Alexander Klozewitz, salesman-astrologer and owner of the **"SYMPTOM HOUSE"A. & S. K. movables agency** give the following statement under full moral, professional and material responsibility.*

I have been asked to reconstruct, retell and analyze, for the needs of the proceedings, two dreams dreamt by the late Mr. Distelli, opera singer, and the late Madam Marquezine Androsovich Lempytzka during the year in which they were murdered, and a bit before and after that. I submit this report on the dreams here for the benefit of the inquest authorities, in the form of two tapes with the following note:

*"In in-depth psychology, the disclosing of a dream's context is a simple, almost mechanical task, which has only preparatory meaning. Putting together a comprehensive text after that, namely the **actual interpretation of the dream,** is a complicated procedure in principle. It*

presumes psychological engrossment, the ability to combine, intuition, insight into the world and people and, most of all, specific knowledges, where familiarity with matters and a certain "intelligence of the heart" are of particular importance." (Helmut Hark, "Lexicon Jungscher Grundbegriffe".)

Besides, it is difficult for me to assume that words can depict something that does not occur linearly nor in the lingual plane in dreams, but is (like in one's thoughts) branched out in all directions and dispersed in the sensual plane and in visual characters, shall we say. Dreams do not inhabit a lingual solution, but drift in a free, timeless space, and as soon as they are transformed into words or writing they lose their compactness and spread out in length. Thus it seems that they last much longer than was actually the case. The entire pages of the two dreams recorded in my report were dreamt only in the duration of several thousand seconds each. A dream, like fear, reaches into depth and width, not length.

Still, I submit to Chief Inspector Stross and the court investigators this attempt to recant and shed light on the one and the other dream in the hope that this will serve judiciary and justice. To give more than that is beyond my ability.

Finally, let me note that Distelli's dream gave me the impression that the dreamer really does inhabit the world at the beginning of the 19th century and experiences everything around his in this world as reality, as though he were truly observing that world through Pushkin's instead of his own eyes. Also, in that dream Distelli experiences at least five different kinds of fear, and so I divided his dream into fears."

Alexander Klozewitz

THE DREAM OF THE LATE OPERA SINGER MR. MATHEAS DISTELLI ON THE DEATH OF PUSHKIN
(IN THE MANNER AND EXTENT IN WHICH A. S. KLOZEWITZ WAS ABLE TO RECANT AND DESCRIBE IT)

The first fear

In the dream of the opera singer Mr. Matheas Distelli Alexander Sergeevich Pushkin appeared as somebody short, very hairy and thin. Distelli did not recognize him, but he somehow realized it was Pushkin as soon as the poet walked over to the window and, with an ancient magical gesture in the sign of Venus, kissed the nail on his thumb, a thumb bearing a large signet ring. It was a stormy night outside and in face of the blizzard the following verses whirled inside the Russian:

> "Skyward soar the whirling demons,
> Shrouded by the falling snow,
> And their plaintive, awful howling
> Fills my heart with dread and woe..."

Inside the window there was another, smaller one called a "fortochka" and Pushkin opened it. Snow hurled into the room.

Then Alexander Sergeevich threw himself into an armchair. A huge hound was sleeping beside him on the divan, a white beauty with a golden head, and on the wall before him hung a portrait of Pushkin's great-grandfather in an officer's uniform from the time of Peter the Great. The great-grandfather was dark-skinned, almost black, he wore a silver wig and a saber under his arm. Pushkin addressed him with the question:

How does one force a demon to enter the room? How does force it to answer one's questions? With what magic can one make it disclose one's future?"

There was a small pile of books lying beside the great-grandfather's left hand in the painting, and beneath the books something that had almost rubbed off the picture, and was barely discernible as some dark object. The great-grandfather's fingers were resting on the book and that unclear object as though he were pointing them out. It seemed like some kind of reply to Pushkin's question that had been "stored" long ago. Alexander Sergeevich, however, knew full well what this object was, for it still existed in his parents' house and stood on the same table that it had been painted on a hundred or so years before. It was the chest of Pushkin's great-grandfather, made of leather with metal reinforcements. Alexander Sergeevich reached for the chest and opened it. In it there were three "voodoo" needles and a purse of old coins from the times of various empires, long since gone out of use. The coins served for the same magical purposes as well.

Opening the chest, Alexander Sergeevich recalled the legends of his great-grandfather and his African origin that had been passed down in Pushkin's family from generation to generation. He also remembered the story of how his great-grandfather had brought the magic needles from Africa to Russia hidden in his hair when he had been caught by slave traders in Africa as a boy and sold to a Count Sava Vladislavich Ragusinsky in Constantinople. The Count was well-versed in magic himself, and sorcery with coins. He must have decided to buy the boy because he recognized the magic needles in his hair. He brought the young black slave to Russia and presented him to Peter the Great, who gave him the name Avram Petrovich Hannibal, put him through military schools and married him to a Russian noblewoman.

"When you wish to find out the truth about yourself," Hannibal used to say, and this was remembered in Pushkin's family, "only your enemy can disclose it to you. If you force him to. And that's what the needles are for."

"Who is a man's greatest enemy?" Pushkin continued with the questions and found the answer himself: undoubtedly the devil. Therefore he should be summoned with the needles and forced to disclose your fate, but how to detect the devil? How do you know you haven't summoned somebody who has never even seen him? So they must first be checked out and then you can pose the question you are interested in. Therefore you must know what the devil is in fact and how to recognize him. People say that men see the devil, and the devil sees God. It is also believed that the tears of the unholy one are not salty. He always adds salt before he eats. His nose is excellent and he can smell his victim from kilometers away. And this, maybe the most important thing, the devil eats as men do, but cannot digest a thing. If he has a glass of red "Tokay" wine, he will pass red "Tokay" wine once more instead of urine. If he eats fish, he will swallow it whole so that it can be laid out onto the table again and served. That is because only the devil does not take part in the global exchange of matter in the Universe.

Such images and memories went through the head of Alexander Sergeevich, who knew full well that the coins in Count Ragusinsky's purse and his great-grandfather's needles were not lying in the same chest by accident.

"Let's get to the point. I hope that my great-grandfather Hannibal's needles still work, combined with the old coins of Count Ragusinsky. A little African magic of Avram Petrovich Hannibal and some Balkan magic of Count Sava Ragusinsky will not be amiss. But I must not forget. I have my great-grandfather's hair. Real African hair. Here is the password for his needles to recognize me..."

And Alexander Sergeevich cut off one of his curls and tossed it into the chest. Then he called out for some Arina Radionovna and told her to fetch three rag dolls from the kitchen, ones with wide skirts used to cover kettles, cookie bowls or baskets of hard-boiled eggs to keep them warm...

When the dolls were fetched, they turned out to be a gray-bearded monk in a wide cassock belted with black cords, a young lady in a wire-supported red skirt with hair of bast and a young man in a tunic with golden hem and a general's epaulettes, bearing a saber.

"Ah, there you are," muttered Alexander Sergeevich and turned towards the bookcase. "Now let me see your destiny. We need a historical event to place you in."

He took out the *History of the Russian State* by Karamsin and the first book of the Venetian history of Russia and Peter the Great, from 1772. He placed them on the table and, with his nail, randomly flipped open the book from Venice first. The year 1599 appeared. The rule of Czar Boris Godunoff.

"Let's see what it says here," he said and began to read:

Boris Godunoff killed prince Dimitri and became Czar, but Godunoff was brought down by some false Dimitri, the Pretender Grishka Otrepyev. Frightened by the military success of the false Dimitri, the Czar became so devastated that he poisoned himself, and the Pretender was pronounced Czar in Moscow and married to a Polish woman, Duchess Marina Mnishek Sendomirska...

Then Pushkin closed the book and concluded, addressing the dolls:

"I've read you enough history. There are things about you that you will have to learn for yourselves. Let's turn to life now. Your life. The Venetian historian claims that the story of Godunoff is a comedy and a tragedy, both. Why not? It has a face and a lining like you dolls do. It's the same in life. The same event unfolds like a comedy in the street and a tragedy in a book. Let us try. First of all, I will furnish the three of you so that you will not be able to escape me any more," he said to the dolls.

And Alexander Sergeevich set to work, writing out rows of figures and lighting a new candle with the old one until dawn. Day was breaking when he carefully tipped out Ragusinsky's old coins from the chest and started examining them and placing some of them aside, counting whether the chosen coins coincided with the calculations that he had been working on all night. Then he grabbed the dolls and said:

"Now to disclose your identities to you and tell you your names."

He placed the rag lad with the saber in front of him first.

"Let's see," he addressed him, "who could you be? Grishka? The name suits you well. The Pretender, then. The false Dimitri. Are you afraid? You are, of course. Here, these three coins go along with you. That's what the calculation says and no hard feelings. Which three coins? I've worked that out as well. One Venetian coin, one Byzantine silver one and half a Dubrovnik dinar. You're not expensive. Let's see... You shall be the false Czar, the Pretender. The Venetian history of Russia says that you disrobed, that is, left the monastic order. It says that you will learn Latin and write letters to the Pope in Rome. It says that, the first time you set foot in the Kremlin, a forceful wind will arise. You shall go to war and an ancestor of mine, one of the Pushkins will help you in this. So, we are old acquaintances. For two centuries now. In the Venetian history it is also written that you shall rule Russia as false prince Dimitri until the rubble drags you from the Czar's palace and kills you on the square. Then a forceful gale will arise once more..."

And Alexander Sergeevich slashed the doll's tunic open with a knife and sewed the three coins into its chest. He sang quietly as he was sewing them in:

> *Peasants here are rich aplenty*
> *Silver they can scarcely measure*
> *To whom the song, to him the treasure...*

"All went smoothly with you, Grishka," added Alexander Sergeevich - and then took hold of the gray-bearded doll in the monk's cassock.

"You, then, are a monk. There were such galore around Czars and courts during the time of Boris Godunoff and Grishka the Pretender. Some were at the Chudovo monastery, where Grishka Otrepyev was a monk as well before he ran off to join the Poles in their march on Moscow. Some of them saw the murder of prince Dimitri at Uglich, ordered by Godunoff. You shall be one of those monks. I'll give you a name. You will be Pyman. With that settled, sit then, brother, and write down my words:

*"This one final recantation
and my chronicle is come to an end..."*

"All right. You can rest now. Let me see your calculation. I cannot get it into my head. Whichever way I look at it, only two coins show up for you. Have you not hidden a few? Here, you can clearly see that it adds up to one Turkish akcha and a German silver taler. Well, it can't be helped."

And under the monastic robe of the rag Pyman Alexander Sergeyevish sewed an akcha and a taler from Count Ragusinsky's purse.

"Now it's your turn, beauty. In your case I know that you have a female number, and it those are always even, so your calculation consists of four coins: one half-silver taler, one gold coin, a Dubrovnik dinar and one akcha."

He picked up the doll in the red, wire-supported skirt, kissed her and undid the buttons. Then he sewed all four of her coins into the hem.

"Your name will be Marina Mnishek Sendomirska. You're a pretty girl. But you're expensive as well," he added, "you shall be a Duchess from Poland and the false Russian Czarina, wife of Grishka the Pretender. When you come to Moscow for the wedding a forceful gale will be blowing. When the rubble kills your pretender husband, you shall slip under the skirt of a nanny, the same kind of skirt as yours, and there you will hide. So says the Venetian book about you..."

After that Alexander Sergeevich addressed all the dolls together:

"To be able to summon you when I need you, I must first picture what you looked like during your lives, all that you did and said. I will do this best if I write a play in which you will all speak and once more find yourselves in the world you used to inhabit. So if I put together a play about Boris Godunoff, the false Czar Grishka Otrepyev and his wife Marina Sendomirska and add something on father Pyman, you will all come to life once more. And so you will be able to respond when I summon you and answer the question that torments me and that I wish to pose to you... So much for tonight!"

On the wall hung a gilded Florentine mirror carved in wood, of which only the gilt remained, for the wood had been eaten away by worms. On the divan slept the hound, and a candle was burning in the room and could be seen in the mirror. Alexander Sergeevich blew into the mirror and the candle was snuffed.

Lying in the dusk before he sank into sleep, he concluded:

"The body learns and grasps more quickly than the soul, for the soul has time, and the body does not."

The Second Fear

The opera singer Distelli dreamt the sequel to his dream about Pushkin such that, as soon as he fell asleep, he saw Pushkin sitting and writing something, and then heard what the Russian was writing:

"I have not read Calderon and Vega, but how great Shakespeare is!" Alexander Sergeevich was writing to his friend Nikolai Rayevski at the moment when he was turning 25. But Shakespeare was not lying in front of Pushkin, beside the recently completed manuscript of the play "Boris Godunoff". On the table before him at that moment there were three kitchen dolls, which had been transformed in the play into the Pretender Grishka Otrepyev, the beautiful Marina and Pyman the monk.

Putting down the only just completed manuscript of "Boris Godunoff", Alexander Sergeevich addressed the dolls with a smile:

"There you are, my dears, and in the midst of tragedy here. For it is a tragedy in the book. But out there, in life, it will be a bit more difficult. Comedy reigns there... But comedy hurts. And how. You will have to hit the road now, and step into life. And life hurts, my pretties. Life smells and hurts. You will feel that on your own hides right away. But you should know how I will summon you when I need you. With the needles!"

And Alexander Sergeevich took Marina, the doll in a red, wire-supported skirt, and stuck one of the African needles with a camel-bone handle into her breast. The sewn-in Byzantine and Venetian coins could be heard crackling beneath the tip. Then he did the same with the doll of Pyman the monk and finally with the doll wearing a saber, the one whose name was Grishka.

"It hurts? Of course it does. But that's it. That's life. But don't be afraid, you can walk now. You will not need me any more, unless I seek you out. You won't need the book either. For I do not need you in the book any more, but in reality. We shall meet in St. Petersburg when I have need of you. I shall summon you from your lives, from the 16th and 17th centuries into my 19th century simply by pricking the dolls with a needle. And then, when I call for you, you will no longer be dolls, but creatures of flesh and blood borrowed from your century into mine. Do not try to get away, for the dolls remain with me, together with the needles. For every insubordination or carelessness of yours I shall push the needle a bit deeper into the body of your doll. And you shall feel it and know how it hurts. So much from me, and now go your ways, creatures of Hades!"

The Third Fear

Distelli's dream continued one winter day when silence became deeper than words, and took place in St. Petersburg. Distelli had never been to that city, but in the dream he somehow knows that it was the Northern Russian capital and that in that dream Pushkin was entering a sled carrying the rag doll in a monk's robe from whose chest an African needle with a camel-bone handle was protruding. The sled stopped before the Monastery of Sts. Peter and Paul.

As he expected, Pushkin saw an old man with a gray beard, wearing a monk's robe, inside the church. His enormous height and slenderness surprised him. He could barely recognize Pyman, who shouted out when he spotted the visitor:

"Bachushka Alexander Sergeevich, finally! What in the name of God are you doing to me?"

"Father Pyman, bless and forgive, if for this there is forgiveness," retorted Alexander Sergeevich and took the monk to a near-by inn. In front of the inn he told the coachman to wait for him to one side, but not to snuff out the lamps on the sled, and walked inside with his guest and ordered a feast - schi, roast duck, mushrooms, a Strasbourg pirogue and two bottles of red "Tokay" wine. The monk kept complaining as they ate.

"Bachushka, you left me neither here nor there and forgot about me. We heard, your Excellency, that you are a poet, they say that you dream in verse, but permit me to ask how long I must now sit around and wait for some kind of resolving?"

"You're not as innocent as you make out to be. You have made war, my friend, under the towers of Kasan and in Lithuania for sure; in all probability you have seen the splendor of the Czar's court..."

"I have. I even knew the Pushkins, your ancestors, and we understood each other well, but you, bachushka, I can barely grasp... You, your grace, are a young man, so permit a monastery hermit and old man to tell you - this trade that you are experimenting on me with is not looked upon kindly by God. It is not. A sin, it is. What are you doing with me, a monk avowed to God? Is that not shameless? And let me ask you one more thing - where are we, bachushka, in the name of God?"

"What do you mean, where are we? In St. Petersburg."

"Never heard of it. Is all this in Russia? I understand nothing of what is said here, and, begging your pardon, I can barely manage to grasp every third word of yours, as if I were catching grasshoppers."

"That is because you speak Ukrainian. And because you come from the time of my great-grandfathers. But it is not your job to understand our times, but to join me in supper and a toast."

Along with words and the roast, Alexander Sergeevich offered his guest red "Tokay" wine until the monk's head fell into his spoon.

Waiting for that precise moment, Alexander Sergeevich led him out onto the snow, to his sled which was standing to one side. They both stopped there in the light of the lamps and Alexander Sergeevich stared at father Pyman, waiting for the critical moment. Then the monk took a deep breath of air filled with tiny snowflakes, hoisted up his robe and took out an enormous member. He urinated so that the horses smelled him and they started spraying the snow beneath their hoofs as well.

But father Pyman was not passing the red "Tokay" wine that they had been drinking that night, but the same as the horses nearby. All was clearly seen in the lamplight.

"Who are you, bachushka?" asked the monk as he lowered his robe, "it is sinful to borrow men from God in this manner, as you have me. Are you the devil?"

"No, father Pyman, I'm not, but I am the one seeking for the devil to ask him a question. And I see you are not the devil either, for if you were the devil you would be urinating red "Tokay" wine instead of what you are passing and the horses as well. So I shall ask you nothing, as my question is for the unholy one and not for you. I was mistaken and forgive me... Pray to the Lord for my soul. Only He knows that I do not do this for spite but out of dire need."

With those words Alexander Sergeevich stepped into his carriage, leaving father Pyman in the snow, and sat back heavily into his seat. Looking out through the window at the monk who was crossing himself swiftly to keep warm and slapping his forehead, waist and shoulder, Alexander took the gray-haired doll in the monk's robe from the pocket on the door of the carriage. He carefully felt for the two coins sewn into it and swiftly removed the African needle of his great-grandfather Hannibal from its breast.

That very instant Pyman, who had been standing alongside the sled, disappeared.

"Pyman is not the devil, then. There are two more to be checked out. Grishka and Marina. Maybe one of them will be the devil. Tough work," concluded Alexander Sergeevich and told the coachman to move on. He was in a hurry and he cursed the servant, forcing him to drive as hard as he could so that they almost broke their necks on their way back home.

The Fourth Fear

It grew even colder in the sequel to Mr. Distelli's dream and the dream became coated in snow. In the midst of snow-bound St. Petersburg in this dream himself, Alexander Sergeevich Pushkin sent candied violets to Duchess Marina Sendomirska with an invitation to dinner at the nearby inn. He had taken the entire top floor of the inn for the night, with two handsome chambers and two bedrooms, and was now waiting for his guest. He ordered a rich dinner, yet with the choice of wine he waited so that Marina could express her wishes as well.

But the guest had still not arrived. The waiters brought in the laid table and plates with the meal - Limburger cheese, pirogue, fish and pineapple, and Marina Mnishek Sendomirska was nowhere to be seen. Taking the opportunity, Alexander Sergeevich removed his signet ring from his thumb and inserted it into the smaller of the two fish lying on a platter. Then he placed the bigger fish on his plate and the smaller one with the ring hidden inside into the plate of his guest. Since she had still not turned up, Alexander Sergeevich took the doll in the red wire-supported skirt, the hem of which was fortified with coins forged from Venice to Constantinople, and pierced the chest of the doll a bit more deeply with his African needle. Several minutes later somebody knocked on the door with three mason strikes, which Alexander Sergeevich recognized and replied in the appropriate manner. He was surprised to see a flushed, gorgeous girl in a red dress and an amber necklace barge into the room.

"Stop, what are you doing to me!" she screamed from the threshold and immediately tore open her dress, showing an unhealed wound beneath the amber necklace.

"Panyi Mnishek! Marina! You speak Lithuanian!" exclaimed Alexander Sergeevich, "and you are crying. I though you would say to me: "Be quiet! You are young and stupid, you will not hunt me down!" How can I order champagne for you if you do not tell me so in Russian? But champagne speaks any tongue. I believe that two bottles of red grape "Veuve Clicquot" would go perfectly with your dress. I have ordered fish and, since you are late, it is already on the table..."

The guest sat down, relaxing a little so that Alexander Sergeevich was finally able to get a good look at her. She was wearing Venetian powder, called "Morticia" there, and thick, wavy hair combed in the fashion of the beauties in Titian's paintings. He struck up a conversation over dinner.

"Have you read "Boris Godunoff" in the "Moscow News" and "Northern Flowers" magazines?"

"No. I read it from your manuscript. In it you say that there is no smile upon my lips. That is not true."

"Why do you think that the Venetian historian called the rule of Godunoff a tragedy and a comedy at the same time?"

"The Czar will be wondering that as well."

"What Czar?"

"How do you mean what Czar? Czar Nikolai the First. Who else?"

"How do you know?"

"That's my business. Do you want a reply or don't you?"

"Let me hear you, beauty. Why did the Venetian historian call the rule of Godunoff both a comedy and a tragedy?"

"Because in the 18th century, the time in which the Venetian historian wrote, such a literary form did exist. It was called a tragicomedy. If you don't believe me, try reading Manuilo Kosachinsky. He has a *"tragicomedy about Czar Urosh"*... Yet I believe that you know all this full well, but have different opinions on tragedy and comedy."

While Alexander Sergeevich was being entertained by this conversation, his guest swallowed the fish whole, together with the ring inside it, right before his very eyes. The plate in front of her remained empty.

"You know, he isn't really from Venice," she chattered and held out her glass for him to pour her some champagne.

"Who isn't from Venice?"

"Your Venetian historian, of course. His name was Zacharia Orfelin."

"How do you know?" Alexander Sergeevich was astounded.

"There is one signed edition of his book that is forbidden."

Pushkin was delighted. His search was going well.

"Such things can only be known by one in cohorts with demons," he thought and poured the Duchess a whole glass of champagne.

They drank up and after another glass Sendomirska announced that she was tired and that she would like to retire, which he approved with relief.

Alexander started from his sleep the following morning with the thought that he had missed something important, that the Duchess had been in boots of the kind that are worn to bed and that he probably should have done something more with her last night. He rushed into her room, but his guest was no longer at the inn, although he had locked the room himself. It was clear that Sendomirska had crept out through his chambers. On a table in her room he found a plate, on it the whole fish that his guest had swallowed the night before at dinner and a glass of red champagne "Veuve Clicquot". The following words had been written on the tablecloth with a finger dipped in champagne: "Greetings from Marina Mnishek".

"This is a good sign," he concluded and took his ring out of the fish with a fork.

"So, I have caught you, beauty! You do not digest food, just as no devil is able to do so."

And he pressed his African needle even deeper into the doll with the wire-supported red skirt. The camel-bone handle almost touched the cloth of the doll.

He did not have to wait long. A knock was heard at the door, and Marina flew into the room.

"What more do you want from me? You could have asked nicely and I would have told you. You didn't have to perform that muddle with champagne and fish. I am Alilat, the devil is my name. Is that what you wanted to know? Since you know who I am now, tell me what I need to do for you to leave me alone?"

"I want to ask you something, dear heart."

"Ask."

How long shall the world I rummage?
To the coach and sled horse trot,
Now a troika, now a carriage,
First in saddle, then on foot?

Neither by my cozy fireside,
Nor midst the graves of mine own kin,
Has my death, then, by the roadside
Dear Lord sent me for my sin?

'Shall I 'neath the horse hooves plunder?
'Neath the wheels and down the ridge?
In a furrow's mud I flounder?
Find my grave 'neath snowy bridge?

"Those are your verses. What do you wish to ask, whether they are good or not? To be honest, they are mediocre."

"Do not jest. That's not what I ask, but the verses ask you something and you must reply to that question."

"You wish to know where and how you shall meet with death?"

"Yes. A net is being woven around me. I must know how to defend myself."

"This that you ask has not been told a living soul since the beginning of time. But I can do something for you in another field. Listen to me and do not reach for your needle right away, for we demons have a needle too. So be wise and take what you are given, in place of that which cannot be given you. Since your question is in verse, my reply shall also be in the domain of poetry. If you agree with this suggestion, take the gun and cloak, and lend me your coat with the golden buttons. It will fit me well. We are going out, then. I shall not be needing guns, but you load yours. You will have to shoot..."

As they walked down the stairs of the inn, Marina explained the goal of their outing:

"You have recently finished the sixth chapter of the novel "Eugene Onegin". There you describe a duel in which your hero killed his friend Lensky. Handsome verses, but you can easily make that scene even better, and this walk could help you in that respect. Here, see the woods along the river, the snow-covered field, it is all like in that novel of yours where you describe the duel. Let us pretend that I am Onegin, and you Lensky. Lie down in the snow and imagine that I have already shot you, and now we come to the improvement of the scene in the novel. For that in the book is but a tragedy, but this here in reality is comedy and it hurts, as you like to put it..."

With those words Marina pushed Alexander Sergeevich and he fell into the snow, at which they both laughed. He noticed then that Marina had a hole in her tongue.

"You see, then, that I can laugh. And as for you, you have in make-believe received a **deadly injury to your stomach**, but you have just enough strength left to rise up onto one elbow and fire at me. Do so now. Aim and fire. Without mercy! May the pain come where it must! Fire!"

Alexander Sergeevich, propped up on one elbow in the snow as though he were truly injured, aimed at Marina's chest thinking: "Le vin est tiré il faut le boire! I'll make you answer my questions." He aimed at the precise spot where the wound from the African needle was, beneath his coat that Marina was wearing. The bullet struck her, but rebounded off the polished button of the coat and flew to the side without harming her.

"That was quite a ricochet!" she exclaimed. "The bullet rebounds off a smooth surface and changes path. Thus you miss your target... That is all that a demoness can do for you concerning your poetic labors, where you are more skillful than she, after all. And now give me the doll, and the needle inside it! I have earned them."

"Why do you think I would want to give you the doll?"

"Because you have received all that can be given in return."

At those words Alexander Sergeevich tossed the doll to Marina. She caught it in midair, tore it apart, threw the money and Hannibal's needle back to Alexander Sergeevich and carried the doll off with her.

The Fifth Fear

In the instant that opera singer Matheas Distelli fell asleep at the oncology ward, in his purchased dream coming from the future that Distelli will no longer be in, Alexander Sergeevich woke up with the thought that the coachman had driven him home too swiftly the night before. He remembered how he had shouted out: "Slow down, fool!" in vain and concluded that his enterprise with the dolls was stuck "between the dog and the wolf".

"Although I did find the devil, the account did not come out into the open. Marina slipped away. Everything somehow turned out to be "neither two nor half". The Duchess did not answer my question. Only that Grishka remains, lest he turns out to be an ace up the sleeve. But he is a dangerous one. He might even draw his saber. That would not be good. I grab the needle, he the saber. But there is cure for that as well..."

Alexander Sergeevich arranged to meet Grishka in a pub in the cellar, one that had a ceiling so low that a saber could not be drawn from its sheath. He took the doll with the general's epaulettes and went to the agreed meeting in the hope that he would meet the devil once more. When the coach stopped in front of the pub, he drove Hannibal's needle a little deeper into the breast of the doll just in case, to "stimulate" the tailless one, if it was he within Grishka's soul. Just in case, he felt for the coins placed beneath the cloth of the doll, placed it into the pocket on the coach door and went to the pub to have a drink and wait for his guest.

He sat there with a glass of lemonade and through the window towards the street it seemed to him that he had seen Grishka pass towards the entrance to the pub. He could plainly see that one of his arms was shorter than the other.

"That's good, if it can be good at all," Alexander Sergeevich whispered and his heart flipped over like a fish, as though it had noticed something that he had missed and was himself not noticing.

"The heart is as mute as a fish, to be true. You are never quite sure what it is that it wants from you," Alexander Sergeevich thought and kept a wakeful eye on the stairs at the entrance. But time passed, and Grishka did not arrive. Then the thought occurred to him that he had seen something strange about Grishka - if indeed that had been him.

"Yes," he recalled, "he has shaven his head! And he rushed down the street in the frost with no cap on. That's the whole point," he finally realized, "Grishka shaved his head to evade the power of magic and break the spell! The fallen, disrobed monk had donned his robe once more, and he had no intention of coming to the pub now but has fled to freedom somewhere. Straight from tragedy to comedy!"

Alexander Sergeevich ran out into the street, looked all around him, but his guest was nowhere to be seen.

Night was already falling, the evening was drowning in the Neva river and he ran to the coach with a chill in his heart, taking the doll with the general's epaulettes from the door pocket to see if the African needle had perchance fallen out of the cloth. The needle was in place, driven in deep, but to his horror Alexander Sergeevich found the stitches on the doll torn apart. Inside it there were none of the coins that he himself has sewn into the doll's tunic. One Venetian one, a Byzantine silver coin and half a Dubrovnik dinar had been stitched into the cloth of the doll. And that money was now gone. He yelled at the coachman, who was sleeping, and asked him if anybody had entered the carriage, but gave up that futile business immediately. Whoever had taken the coins, the coachman who had drunk them right away and was now sleeping, near senseless, or Grishka, who had snuck in and stolen the coins from his own doll, it all amounted to the same. The African needle was still inside the doll, but there were no more coins beneath its skirts, meaning that he who had taken the Venetian, Byzantine and Dubrovnik coins while the needle was inside the doll had sentenced Grishka to an eternity of neither life nor death, between tragedy and comedy... Unles Grishka was the devil.

"But that I shall never know..."

With those thoughts Alexander Sergeevich concluded his search for the unholy ones, took the whip from the hands of the drunken coachman, struck the horses and they started off on their own, lulling him into a doze. Midnight struck from the tower of Sts. Peter and Paul and the horses were frightened by the clanging, rushing homewards even faster. At the end of the dream. The horses' bells chimed again and again in a whisper:

At-the-end-of-so-li-tude-begins-death, at-the-end-of-so-li-tude-begins-death...

POST SCRIPTUM

──────── ♦ ────────

Dreams never have titles. In both of the cases recorded here I gave names to the dreams. Now I would like to draw the attention of Chief Inspector Stross to the fact that I named Distelli's dream "The Dream on Pushkin's Death" because this dream foretells the poet's death quite accurately, though it does not speak of it.

As is known to experts in this field, Pushkin died on November 10th 1837 from a wound inflicted upon him in a duel with the French emigrant J. Dnates, who had shot first. Eyewitnesses claim that, with a deadly injury to his stomach, the poet lay in the snow and, supporting himself on one elbow, fired his shot, which struck Dantes in the chest, but it hit a metal button and ricocheted off to the side without even harming Pushkin's opponent.

I make note of this for it can also be of significance in the Distelli-Lempytzka case that Chief Inspector Stross is investigating.

THE SECOND PART OF THE REPORT SUBMITTED BY ALEXANDER KLOZEWITZ AT THE REQUEST OF THE COURT
(TAPE 2)

Submitting to the Court authorities this report on the dream of the late Madam Marquezine Androsovich Lempytzka, set forth in the form of an audio recording at their request and the request of Chief Inspector Eugene Stross, I would like to make several notes.

At a certain point before the middle, this "dream of Madam Lempytzka about footsteps", as it may be called, begins to act strangely. It branches out into three flows that Madam Lempytzka dreams as the same time. One of these three flows she experiences as an androgyne being, the other as a woman and the third as though she were a man. It might be most accurate, in fact, if we were to say that this becomes a dream on three floors. The meaning of this three-pronged fork, this three-story dream at the end of the dream of Madam Lempytzka should be inquired of somebody experienced in in-depth psychology, for I am not a psychiatrist, and therefore am unfit to enter into such issues. I am a simple salesman.

Finally, I am obliged to note that dreams are a strange matter. Another person would certainly describe this dream of Madam Lempytzka in quite a different manner and perhaps allocate the names and roles within it differently, for like in every dream, the characters in this one are also doubled or divided. I must also mention that Lempytzka received her dream more by hearing that in the form of pictures.

Although I submit this report and the tape with the audio recording with the best intentions, my limitations in this area are unquestionable."

Alexander Klozewitz

THE DREAM OF THE LATE MADAM MARQUEZINE ANDROSOVICH LEMPYTZKA ABOUT FOOTSTEPS

(IN THE MANNER AND EXTENT IN WHICH A. S. KLOZEWITZ WAS ABLE TO RECANT AND DESCRIBE IT)

"We do not own houses, they own us"- with this sentence spoken aloud begins the dream of Madam Lempytzka, who in it immediately turned into a boy. In that dream the boy lived in the large house of his parents which owned him. He slept upstairs in a small room located inside another, larger one - the dining-room. It was a room within a room, then. In it, apart from the bed, there was a pillow chest; the chest was decorated with two leather handles and a porcelain apple on the lid.

The small room had two windows with pretty curtains through which the family and guests could be seen as they entered the dining-room, and the mother could check if the boy had fallen asleep at night. If he was holding onto one of the leather handles of the chest, she would conclude that the boy was sleeping.

But sometimes the boy was not asleep, though he was firmly gripping a handle of the pillow chest. He was listening with his eyes closed. It was always the same. Against the windowless wall of the room a huge cupboard was located.

Like a third room within a room. And sometimes footsteps could be heard from inside it. Somebody was walking in the cupboard of the small room... This did not happen always. But it could be heard quite clearly.

Since this lasted for years, the boy started school in the meanwhile and learned to tell the days of the week. And so he concluded that the footsteps could be heard on Sundays, but some other times as well. He struggled for a long time to figure out if they were male or female footsteps. Or both male and female. And where they went when they died down. They had heels, but not very pointy ones like mother's heels were. So the footsteps were not his mother's. Sometimes these footsteps behind the double doors of the wooden giant were close together and restless, and once they walked away slowly, only to break out into a trot in the distance. The boy was scared and sat up in bed, but he did not know what he could say to the grownups. And so he was silent about the footsteps in the cupboard.

That cupboard had a large keyhole and it was locked. The boy's clothes and things were not inside it. Sometimes the boy peered into the cupboard through that keyhole, but inside it was a dusk that smelled of tobacco. The cupboard also had two small windows closed with bars made of interwoven horseshoes.

A long time went by before the boy realized that, apart from Sundays, the footsteps could be heard on holidays as well. As though somebody was using his days of leisure to come and stroll through the cupboard in his room. One evening the boy saw moonlight slowly spread across the cupboard. And seep into it through the keyhole. His hairs on end, he drew up a chair, climbed onto it and peeked inside through the barred window. He saw nothing. He poked his finger into the dark with the fear that something would bite him and felt a wooden shutter behind the bars. He took a pencil and pushed the shutter ajar. Still he could see nothing because there was a glove hanging on the bars from the inside. He repeated the procedure with the other shutter. No glove was hanging there. Inside, by the light of the moon, a single, so astounding thing could be seen that the boy almost fell off the chair in surprise. A tree was growing inside the cupboard. Its white-black leaves could plainly be seen in the moonlight thin as silence that reigned within the cupboard. A real, live fruit tree was growing there with transparent red wild cherries that seemed as of glass... And a huge white hound was sleeping beneath the tree.

The terrified boy never again dared peek into the cupboard, but matters got worse one evening when from inside it he could plainly hear water trickle, gurgle and bubble, and a quiet female voice sing the song "Green Protects from the Rain"... After every verse the voice would quietly hiccup and, after a brief hesitation, start singing once more. All the fluids in the boy were in a turmoil because of that voice. As if called out for, all the juices in him responded and boiled. Secretions frothed within his body, warm blood surged through him bearing with it like a shadow some other network, not of blood circulation but something much, much older, the flow of something ancient that has been running through human bodies for millions of years. In the same instant the saliva beneath his tongue became as honey, the hot tears in his throat bitter, his eyes were stung by salty sweat with the stench of a mare and the taste of his male seed turned into that of female milk...

Like a sleepwalker, the boy went up to the cupboard and whispered into the keyhole:

"What are you doing here?"

The voice inside was cut short as though bitten off. The boy tried once more, indecisively:

"Hey, who are you?"

The unfamiliar voice retorted in a whisper that was closer than the boy had expected:

"I'll tell you, so you don't say that I didn't later on."

"Why don't you let me in there with you?"

"What would I need you for?"

And the song was heard once more, quietly, with occasional hiccups. In between the verses the girl inside sneezed smelling of fish, scratched, coughed in a particular way: always twice, quietly, then loudly, cursed horses, spat with hacking, whistled through her teeth, jingled keys as though she were trying to unlock the cupboard from the inside, or to lock it... And all that as she sang.

Then through the keyhole somebody from inside the cupboard blew a stream of pipe tobacco with the aroma of wild cherries and honey into the boy's eyes. And that was all. With that smell, terrified and exhausted he fell asleep halfway to the bed, lying down on the sheep-fleece rug. An unknown creature whispered several words into his ear while he slept. He did not understand them, but he memorized them and repeated them from time to time so as not to forget them:

> *At a time like this, oh Lord,*
> *Free us of our faith*
> *And receive us unto Thee as prey.*

Δ

As noted at the beginning of this report, Madam Lempytzka's dream branches out here into three separate flows.

THE BRANCH THAT MADAM LEMPYTZKA DREAMT AS AN ANDROGYNE BEING

The boy is sitting at the table in his room, the cupboard from which he can sometimes hear the trickle of water is behind his back, and into the room steps Oharaska, his cousin. She is 14, he about half her age, but he does not know how old they are. It is afternoon, time flows making curves and loops. In the house of the boy's parents everybody is enjoying this period of rest after their meal, and Oharaska is carrying a tray with a glass of raspberry juice and a bowl of porridge. She makes it herself and before she places the glass and the bowl in front of the boy her mouth spreads into a broad smile full of teeth and tongue.

The boy understands the meaning of that smile full well and shouts out, horrified:

"No! No! No!" but does not move from the chair, as though he were bewitched...

— — — — — — — — — — — — — — — — —

The boy did not understand what was happening with him those days and weeks, he bit his toenails and when he had gnawed them to the quick, he listened in horror from his bed as guests gathered at the round dining-room table in the evening...

One evening already seated there were his mummy, Eleanor Cikindyal, in whose bun silver needles and hairpins rattled as she spoke, the beautiful Mrs. Tessa Pokumica, who scratched as she walked like birds scratch with their beaks in flight and her husband, Mr. Pokumica, who still paid her by the hour to look at her naked. He sometimes had two profiles at his disposal, the left one auburn, the right one dark. Old Duchess Marina Sendomirska Ipsilanty barged noisily into the dining-room, shouting from the doorway:

"Many kisses, many kisses!" signifying that she had no intention of kissing those present individually in greeting. She was carrying her fan, in her accent there was a hint of Polish and Lithuanian, and, as usual, she was under Venetian powder. She was always very careful to wear more rings than she did years and she went visiting with her three lovers, three brothers from Missolungi who were able to say their surname Prodromidis in all five of the holy languages. The Prodromidises looked upon the world through Missolungi fog, and every year at Easter they would receive gifts from Duchess Sendomirska Ipsilanty. Those gifts were always the same. To each a pair of mason gloves of light yellow deerskin, and a portrait that Duchess Sendomirska Ipsilanty would commission to be painted in oil. Those portraits were painted at the bottom of small medallions (in five copies each) by a craftsman skilled at painting schooners and barges on the river, and they were made so that their owners could present them to their business associates together with their cards. Namely, Duchess Sendomirska Ipsilanty did not believe in photographs. She would also bring the boy a specially prepared gift: from an ice-cream maker she commissioned icons to be etched into lollipops, and so the boy would receive at Easter a lollipop with the image of St. Paraskeva or Archangel Michael. They were very sweet by taste. The Holy Mother Paraskeva tasted of rum at that, and Archangel Michael complete with sword had a lovely aroma of vanilla.

But a lollipop in bed was small comfort for what had yet to be endured. Listening to the chattering of the guests, the boy in his own bed and somebody else's dusk was biting his toenails for he was consumed with horror of what was to take place out there.

In the middle of the dining-room there was a huge, round table, and as soon as the cloth was removed from it the boy knew what was to come. The table was put together without nails and the guest would gather around it to invoke spirits.

"Whom shall we invoke tonight?" asked Mrs. Cikindyal as she sat down at the table, "perhaps the late doctor Isidore? He might be able to help me. It seems that I have trodden on some unholy force. When I get up in the morning I find the door of the glassware cabinet open, the one on my father's library gaping wide and that of the candy bar ajar..."

"Somebody has cast a spell on me as well," interjected Mrs. Tessa, "I find my stockings tied in a knot every morning. Lord help us!"

"I've long since been meaning to ask Dimitri if there were female Masonic lodges in his day and whether my deceased has attended their gatherings," added Mrs. Eleanor Cikindyal - at which her boy in his room pricked up his ears, realizing that this "spying after death" referred to his late father.

"Does the fact that Dimitri is member of the lodge not prevent him from discussing such matters?" remarked the Duchess.

"Who's to know," snapped the eldest Prodromidis brother disinterestedly, "they are probably not obliged to keep those secrets any more after death..."

"In that case," accepted Mrs. Tessa, "let's see if Dimitri is available tonight. What do you say we ask the pot?"

"That's not a bad solution," said Mrs. Cikindyal, took a hidden rapier out from behind a painting, checked to see if it was sharp and placed it on the round table, and set a clay pot on the tiny heating plate beside the window. When the water started boiling, everybody pricked up their ears, and through the bubbling of the water the pot could be heard pronouncing a word.

"Vic! Vic! Vic!" came from the pot.

"Who is this Vic now?" Mrs. Tessa was astounded and looked at herself in the mirror with her beautiful eyes.

"We called for no such person," said one of the lovers of Duchess Sendomirska.

"Don't speak so of names," chided Mrs. Tessa. "Names are somewhat like bottles in which the essence of the persons bearing them are preserved, they keep something like homunculus..."

At that moment another chair appeared at the table, completely transparent, as if of glass, and a sitting male figure started to materialize upon it. First a sleeve with a strange smell, and then the entire thick, winter clothing, although it was spring outside. The clothing looked smarter than the one wearing it. The hand was writing something on the table.

"Who are you?" asked Mrs. Cikindyal.

"Don't you recognize me, mother dear? I am your Vic."

"I don't know any Vic!"

"I wouldn't accept any uninvited guests into my home if I were you, Mrs. Eleanor," complained the youngest Prodromidis.

"Who did you say you were?" repeated the hostess.

"But I am your son, Victor!"

"Dear Lord, what is he on about? My Victor is barely seven years old and is sleeping behind this window in his room. And you, you are a deceiver and this shall be seen immediately!"

With those words Mrs. Cikindyal grabbed the rapier and drove it into the breast of the man representing himself as Vic.

Everybody in the dining-room cried out, but Vic smiled unharmed, for the blade passed through him as it would through wind and struck the back of the nearest chair, from which the eldest lover of Duchess Sendomirska leapt as if scalded.

"I believe, mother dear, that our pots have gotten a bit mixed up," said Vic peaceably.

"How so?" beautiful Mrs. Tessa spoke up, terrified, and Mrs. Cikindyal, still stunned, by force of habit made the sign of the cross with the rapier over the mock wound that she had inflicted upon the stranger.

"You really seem not to be from this world? Do you have an explanation for all this?" she asked.

"I do," retorted Vic, "the explanation is simple: you did not invoke me, but I invoked you. You are the spirits, not I. That's why you cannot harm me with that rapier of yours, which, by the way, has long since been gone from this room, as well as the painting you have been hiding it behind."

"And where is it that you invoked us from, young man?" asked Mrs. Tessa.

"Ah, that's what I'd like to know. But how should I know where the dead come from when they are invoked? Surely you should know this better yourselves."

"Dead? You say that we are dead?"

"Well I certainly am not. You, aunt Tessa, died in 1898, two years after your husband; you, Mr. Prodromidis, although youngest, died, if you'll pardon my saying so, before your eldest brother, and only uncle Harris, your middle brother, is still alive. That's why only he isn't here... Besides, after the acclaimed death of Duchess Sendomirska he inherited the most precious of her rings, the one that whispers. He says that she gave it to him on her deathbed, although I don't believe that you, Duchess, have really died. That's fuzzy in my memory somehow... You, forgive me for having to say so, are neither here nor there..."

"Oh, the cheek!" cried the Duchess, "he lies the moment he opens his mouth! Are you, Eleanor, going to permit guests to be treated in this manner in your home? This is unheard of! Since you're like that, here, I'll tell you, you shall die of a firearm twice, but once in your sleep, as a man, and the second time awake as a woman!"

"Dear aunt Marina, that only means that I have not been killed yet, that I'm alive, and was therefore able to invoke you."

"And how can the dead be invoked, according to your knowledge and skill?" Mrs. Cikindyal broke into the discussion.

"'To ease your consciences, I have to tell you," concluded Vic, "that the dead cannot be summoned from the other world. Although spirits have always existed, before birth and after death, they can be invoked only from some day and year that they lived in, and not from the time when they were yet unborn or already dead. And so I invoked you. I believe that this is your year 1881, the month of May. My seventh year, in fact. Here, with me, it is quite a different year and another century, it's winter, that's why I'm dressed this way..."

"That's enough of this game!" Mrs. Cikindyal interrupted the tale. "If things are as you present them, what about the real Victor then, who is sleeping here in the next room, which you can check for yourself. You only need peek through that window."

"There's no need for me to check, mother dear, I remember how I used to sleep in that little room while you invoked spirits and let me tell you, for I can recall, what I am doing now there in my bed and in my seventh year. I am not sleeping in bed at the moment, but am biting my toenails out of fear. Besides, grownup as I am, on Sunday and holiday evenings I sometimes come in my mind to the cupboard in the nursery to take a look through the bars at myself as a child sleeping in that bed..."

"Whatever you might babble on about," interrupted Mrs. Cikindyal, "I, to tell you the truth, do not believe that I have died, and that's that... Strange... As a child you weren't as ugly as you are now... Who would have thought you'd look like this... If it is you at all... See the size of your shoes. Cats could bear kittens in them... But, tell us at last, what was it that you wanted from us, come out into the open, if you please! Why did you, as you say, invoke us?"

"By mistake, mother dear, by mistake."

"And who was it that you wished to invoke?" beautiful Mrs. Tessa barged into the conversation.

"Dear aunt Tessa, after your death, and I was in love with you while you were beautiful, and you were beautiful until deep into your old age, well, after your death I took your things, trinkets, scent bottles, powders and blushes, tissues and eyebrow pencils, fake moles, scissors and gloves with embroidered rings, the eyelash-curling device, a whole bunch of such shiny objects and I carry them with me throughout the world now, packed in a green chest bound by leather belts... I look them over sometimes and I can tell you that they still smell of your hair from time to time. But you are not the one that I wished to see tonight."

"Whom, then?" demanded Mrs. Tessa with disappointment.

"For your sake I shall tell you whom I wanted to invoke when I received you by mistake. Listen, then.

"If you are going to invoke one of the spirits, you can also invoke somebody who has not yet been, but is about to be born. He is also in that endless other world of yet unborn souls, and those laid to rest. As souls cannot be invoked from their unbeing, but only from some point in time when they did exist, the souls from the Universe of the unborn must be invoked in the only possible form in which we, the living, can notice them and reach them with our senses, and that is their physical existence in the womb of their mother. I, aunt Tessa, wished to invoke such a soul from the Universe of the future, as yet unborn, but embodied, whose arrival in this world is expected soon by her mother. I wished to invoke this unborn being to find out if I was its father and which part of the world it was in, but I erred somewhere in the invoking and received you... That's all. But, as long as you're all here, let me take advantage of this meeting."

And Vic turned to Mrs. Cikindyal with the words:

"I would like to ask you something, mother dear, which I did not have the courage to ask during your lifetime."

"What might that be?"

"Do you know who was in the cupboard in my nursery? Whose footsteps were those that I could hear inside it? There was some female voice that quietly sang "Green Protects from Rain..." And a tree was growing there."

"You're babbling again, my child!" retorted Mrs. Cikindyal, "besides, if we are to believe you and the words you just spoke, those were your own footsteps. You yourself said that you still come sometimes, grownup as you are, and peek at the children's bed from the cupboard... Nonsense. You should not concern yourself with that, my child. It's not healthy. You know how they say: a priest at the anvil and a blacksmith at the book always err..."

At these words the pot on the table turned upside-down of its own accord, after which Vic disappeared from the sight of the present company.

THE BRANCH THAT MADAM LEMPYTZKA DREAMT AS A FEMALE PERSON

The boy that Madam Lempytzka became as soon as she fell asleep was no longer small. This time Madam

Lempytzka encountered Master Victor Cikindyal in her dream as a tall young man with a well-cooked and very thick gaze, who was on his way to continuing his studies in Grenoble. He already possessed a tree that shed tears upwards, the very kind that Lempytzka had never had.

As soon as she found him in this town in her dreams, Cikindyal stopped at an inn, ordered turkey with wild cherries and "Bordeaux" with "Camembert", which was bad for him, to be true, but he could not resist. Sitting beside his two green chests bound with leather belts, he reached for the newspaper in a reed frame from the hook and opened it at the advertisement page. He was looking for rooms for rent. The following ad immediately attracted his attention:

For rent: Bathroom with a view of the river and sleeping niche.

Everybody usually offered rooms with a bathroom, but here it was the other way around. Once more, he could not resist and went to see what was in fact being offered. The bathroom had a balcony with a garden set of table and chairs, a crystal apple instead of a handle, a glass dome from which a Venetian chandelier was suspended, a Voltaire armchair "with ears" in mauve velvet, a Persian carpet and a stone tub at the end of which stood a marble female bust. Fully dressed he lay down into the empty tub and looked through the window. He could see the river. The bathroom really did overlook the Isere. It had something that resembled an entrée, and inside it, behind a curtain, he discovered a huge double door. It led towards the other part of the house that was forbidden and was not for rent. In that old-fashioned, wide door was a folding bed. So the bathroom really did have a sleeping niche, quite literally. He did not hesitate for a moment. He rented it and moved in.

Young Cikindyal traveled to the university by street car, furnished as though it were a room and lacking only coffee being served. In this street car one evening on his way home from classes he experienced a miracle. At the park in the center of town the street car slowed down extremely, almost stopping, music could be heard and all the passengers rushed to the windows to catch a glimpse, and so did Cikindyal as well. It would have been better if he hadn't.

In the park there was a tiny restaurant and the guests outside were dancing the tango. But what a tango. Victor Cikindyal had never seen nor dreamt anything like it. The movements of the ten or so couples were better than the music and that could clearly be felt inside the vehicle, where the music was muffled. He immediately leapt breathlessly out of the moving street car, but he wasn't the only one to do so. Other passengers descended as well to sit in the restaurant and watch the fairytale scene. As if drugged, he found a place at one of the tables, upon which an empty glass with the imprint of female lips was standing. The edges were slightly chewed off. He stared fervently at the dance and his gaze came to rest upon a male couple that was dancing a "bloodthirsty" tango. That male couple was perfect, and nothing in their movements seemed the least bit unnatural. They took turns leading, first one then the other, taking on the female, then the male role in the dance. Only later, when the young men separated in the middle of the dance and found their female partners once more, did Vic notice the two of them as well. In fact, the first thing he noticed was the red dress on one of the two girls. The dress had the inscription:

"I CARRY THE ONE CARRYING ME"

That dress really did carry the girl through the dance, not she the dress. The girl had a gilded belt beneath her breasts instead of at her waist and lacquered shoes with red soles that could be seen at every turn. Over the shoulder of her young man she smoked a long, thin pipe throughout the dance. When the tango ended, her escort brought her to the table at which Cikindyal was sitting, bowed thanking her for the dance and returned to his own table. The girl with the pipe turned towards Cikindyal and said to him in his native tongue:

"What are you doing here?"

He stood up, confused as a river at its delta. He watched her lips sprinkled with multicolored glitter as they gleamed in the sunlight like a couple of fish.

"How did you know where I was from?"

"How did I know? It was easy, I could tell by the way your buttons are sewn on. But you can stay at the table under two conditions: first, that you breathe not a single word more and second, that you buy me an ice-cream. One in a twist of pastry will be fine."

He went to fetch the ice-cream, and when he returned he found the pipe lying on the table. The girl was dancing again, and with another cavalier this time... It seemed as though her movements were in command of the music and that the music was following them, not the other way around. In passing she took the cone from Cikindyal's hands, licked and returned it to him without interrupting the steps that were actually a game of chess against the one with his arms around her.

"Go ahead and take a lick," she told him, flopping into the chair when the music died down.

"Is it hard to dance as prettily as you do?"

"The hardest thing is adjusting to the louts you have to dance with. Some are like fir-wood, they flame up quickly and turn into smoke, and then they are nothing but trouble; others are like junipers, they smell nice, but that's all; the third are like the Turkey tree, stable, but raw, there is no fire in them, some are as thick as a beech, others deep-rooted as an oak. The best ones are mixed."

"And which kind am I?"

"You're not very sweet. You could be something like a wild cherry. I won't know until I dance with you."

"I don't know how to dance."

"I knew it. There's been enough dancing anyway. It makes the soles of my feet burn... Do you know what all these lady dancers will do tonight?"

"No."

"They'll wash their feet in cold milk."

She slipped the sandals off her feet, shoved them into his hands for him to carry and got up with the words:

"Do you have cold milk?"

"I do."

"Is it far away?"

"What?"

"You are silly. You're bathroom, I'm asking if it's far away?"

"No. It's quite nearby," he retorted and they started off.

As soon as they found themselves in the rented premises of Master Cikindyal, the girl bit his finger and before his astounded eyes dropped all her clothing, grabbed a bottle of milk from the fridge and jumped into the bathtub slamming the door with the crystal apple instead of a handle behind her.

Victor stretched out onto the bed, and the gurgle of various liquids could be heard from the bathroom along with the girl's quiet singing that was interrupted from time to time by a hiccup. The song was somehow familiar to him, and he seemed to be able to make out the words: "Green Protects from the Rain"... And then he realized at last. The song that the girl was singing was a tango.

Then he called out to her through the door, without rising from the bed:

"Hey, who are you?"

"I'll tell you, so you don't say that I didn't later on. Zla-ti-ja!"

And the song was heard once more, quietly, with occasional hiccups. In the bathroom the girl was singing with pauses, interrupting the song, sneezing, scratching, coughing through the tango in a particular way: always twice, quietly, then loudly, cursing horses, spitting with hacking, whistling through her teeth, jingling keys as though she were trying to lock the bathroom from the inside. She finally asked Vic to fill and bring her a lit pipe. As he was approaching, he could feel her female moisture on his lips, and smell the scent of tobacco with the aroma of wild cherries and honey. That smell made all the fluids inside of Vic cry out in a turmoil. As if called out for, all the juices in him began to boil. Secretions frothed within his body, warm blood surged through him bearing with it like a shadow some other network, not of blood circulation but something much, much older, the flow of something ancient that has been running through human bodies for millions of years. In the same instant the saliva beneath his tongue became as honey, the hot tears in his throat bitter, his eyes were stung by salty sweat with the stench of a mare and the taste of his male seed turned into that of female milk... Then he entered the bathroom.

Δ

In the morning Cikindyal asked Zlatija:
"Why don't you stay with me?"
"What would I want you for? Besides, I have two husbands already, the first and the second, who is a "second hand" husband. I can't stand them. I am always turned towards the future as my main enemy. To defend myself from it I keep foretelling, letting my intuitions hunt through the invisible tomorrow, I am forced to prophesy, to forecast horrified of all that could happen and that will inevitable take place in that tidal wave of future ageing, my own and that of others, for I know that old age is not just the one, but that I shall have countless of them. The only way to outsmart the future is to get pregnant. My husbands, though, do not understand my fears. What do they care for a child as yet unmade, for an America that has not been discovered? They live in today and will not hear of anything in that still unreached continent of the future, my husbands are not interested in terra incognita."
"Where are those husbands of yours?"
"Downstairs, in front of your building. Both of them. They are waiting for me to come down."
"How do they know where you are?"

"They always know where I am. You would, too, if you were one of my husbands. But you aren't and so goodbye, dear heart! Let me comfort you in parting, I shall tell you a secret."

"Go ahead."

"Maybe you made me a baby tonight. Maybe."

Δ

Master Cikindyal learned to dance the tango perfectly, he regularly went to the park in which the lovers of this dance gathered, bought ice-cream for the dancers, but he never met Zlatija again. And she was the only one he was looking for. He thought:

"The people that we meet every day for a long time are harder and harder for us to see as time goes by and in the end we remember them and keep them in our minds as though they were ten years younger. As though they were still the same persons spotted for the first time and gazed upon long ago. It's the same with love. Zlatija is still dancing her tango there in the Grenoble park to me, although she is no longer there."

He loved her backwards through time, more and more often imagining earlier moments one before the other, towards the beginning of their relationship, which reached its climax at the very first time his eyes met her, when he read the following words on her dress:

"I CARRY THE ONE CARRYING ME"

Now, remembering her that way, her and her red dress, he realized that Zlatija had been pushed into her female nature as into that dress, perhaps against her will, but there had been nothing that she could do about it. And so in his thoughts and memories he would come to her smile, which created something like a pretty spasm in her curves, as though laughter hurt her.

"Secrets are older than the truth," he thought and searched first for the unknown woman with whom he had spent the night, remembering the touch of her hands in the dark, as though there had been three of them - two warm ones and one cold - and then when he did not find her, he began to search year by year in every possible way for the child that he might have had with her.

"Time exists only in calendars, everybody has his own time in life," he thought as he searched. And he never found her or the child. Maybe that was taken care of by her two husbands, the first and the second, who was a "second hand" husband. Maybe.

THE BRANCH THAT MADAM LEMPYTZKA DREAMT AS A MALE PERSON

This branch of Madam Lempytzka's dream is really more in the form of sounds than actual images. The man appearing in that dream is terribly tired, lazy, or very old so he is writing a letter slowly. Lempytzka can plainly hear what is being written in her dream, but she cannot hear his voice.

Graz, August 2nd, c.y.

Dear and much revered Miss Euphrasia,

I am only now replying to your two kind letters, since I am too old for nice and joyous things as well, let alone the others, which do not, fortunately, include your letters. To the contrary, they gave me pleasure, I - permit me to say so straight away - liked and respected your late father Major Cikindyal dr. Victor, and you have come to the right person concerning the sad matters that you wish to know about him. He was a very reserved gentleman, a strong and meek man, he liked bread kneaded with tobacco and prayed to the water that he was about to drink...

But we had better start from the beginning, from your first letter, then. Madam Zlatija, whom I did not have the honor of knowing, was right when she told you that it was better to have three fathers than one. Still, I was touched by that part of the letter in which you say that you went to Grenoble sometimes to tango in the park in the hope that you might meet your true father there. Unfortunately, it was too late by then. And so you are correct when you write that you never met him and that you did not find out he was your father until he was no longer among the living.

However, let me tell you now that he was not buried in that grave on Socha that you mention in your first letter, although the military cross of that grave still bears his name and surname with the correct date of birth and incorrect date of death. You ask me how I know? Here's how. During the military actions on Socha I accompanied Major Cikindyal as his orderly the year that is listed as second on the said military cross. During the military actions in that area we passed by a grave. We stopped beside it and Major Cikindyal read his own name on the cross.

"How could such an error be possible, Major, sir?" I asked, and, not the least bit surprised, he gave me the following reply:

"It is not an error. An old Duchess prophesied long ago that I would die twice. Once as a man, the second time as a woman. And so it isn't strange that I shall have two graves. This could be my female grave."

So much about the first grave of your father, dear and revered Miss Euphrasia.

Now we come to your second letter. Let me reply to your main question of where your father, Major Cikindyal, is buried. I was present not only as his orderly, but as somebody who had the luck to be of the same civilian profession as doctor Cikindyal, and so I helped him in his unmilitary duties as well, which he did not neglect even during the war. I remember that we were stationed in the Statenberg castle and that the Major received reports from the commanders of the units under him there. It was afternoon, Major Cikindyal had gathered us in the library of the castle and he was receiving the reports at a huge renaissance table upon which the maps of the war regions on the Piave and Socha were spread out. He was on his feet, for he had strong, chronic pains and could neither sit nor stand, and so, as others spoke, he paced the room. Sometimes he would, while constantly following what was being said and giving instructions and remarks, look over the books on the castle shelves and take out one of them, and then return it, or place it on the table before him. Besides, I knew that apart from military maps he had other things on the table that were used for his skilled research, which he considered to be more important that the war work. The more so because he knew in advance that the war was lost and everything that he did as Major he performed by force of some accustomed habit without much conviction in the purposefulness of the work that he always undertook extremely conscientiously, nevertheless.

And so, apart from the military maps, on the table before him that afternoon there was a German edition of the final tome of Gibbon's book "The Decline and Fall of the Roman Empire", and several maps and panoramas of Constantinople with images of the town before and after the Turkish conquering. These were:

"Byzantium nunc Constantinopolis" - a map published between 1566 and 1574, by "Lorentz & Keil, Libraires de S.M.I. Le Sultan".

"The Delineation of Constantinople as it stood in the Year 1422 before it fell under the domination of the Turks", from Du Fresne Lib. 1 p. 1

"Constantinopel" - a German undated edition representing Constantinople from the time before the Turkish conquest.

Major Cikindyal copied from that German edition, and another, anonymous one colored later on, into his papers the symbols placed on all the town towers of Byzantine Constantinople:

This drawing was accompanied by his note: "on all the Constantinople towers there is a shield with four letters around a cross, the elements of the Serbian crest. Whether because the origin of the later Byzantine emperor was..."

These were the last words written by Major Cikindyal. The following day a command to move out was issued, and we entered a battle in which the Major was struck down before my very eyes. He was buried there where he fell and his grave can still be found today beneath the military cross of an army that no longer exists. He died in a state that exists no more and now his grave is in some other state. The fruit tree that he was buried under still stands over his grave. Every year it is full of red wild cherries, transparent as of glass... If Miss Euphrasia should desire to visit the grave of her father, I, despite my years, am prepared to escort her there...

Since the wartime heritage of Mr. Cikindyal remained in my possession, I found among his papers an unusual piece of writing, and it belongs to this letter as well. Namely, in childhood your father dreamt that somebody was whispering a prayer into his ear. He recalled this prayer and wrote it down, and I took the liberty of placing it, inscribed upon a plaque, onto the cross above his grave. The prayer is as follows:

At a time like this, oh Lord,
Free us of our faith
And receive us unto Thee as prey.

EPILOGUE OR THE "BLUE BOOK"

———— ♦ ————

Catalogue of all hundred endings
of this novel

Δ

WARNING:

Just as smoking is bad for your health,
so is the reading of a hundred endings
of the same book.
It is almost like gaining one hundred
deaths instead of one.

Since Erlangen was sentenced to prison for the murder of Madam Marquezine Androsovich Lempytzka, and Alexander Klozewitz duly paid the allocated fine for the illegal gain of profit in the case of the monetary claims of late Madam Lempytzka's inheritor, these cases could have been considered closed.

But Chief Inspector Eugene Stross was not a man to spend the entire night on the same pillow. He had at least three of them. Therefore Mr. Eugene Stross made notes in his diary, which was some kind of a private inquest protocol, about cases that had officially been closed long ago. Two cases in particular attracted his attention: the murder of Isaiah Cruise at the hippodrome which had remained unsolved, and the Lempytzka case.

Most of the notes made by Mr. Stross were undated so it was hard to determine their chronology. A little more should be said about one exception and a note with a date. The diary of Mr. Stross was cut short before the book was filled, and the last note was written on November 1st 2003, which is, as we know, the date of the murder of Chief Inspector Eugene Stross. During one arrest attempt the suspect tried to flee, Inspector Stross drew his gun, but before he managed to shoot the mobile phone in his pocket rang, and he received a knife in his back. An accomplice of the suspect threw the knife from quite a distance. The murderer was never caught. The knife was sharpened for the left hand, meaning that it had been thrown by a left-handed person. In the police files of former convicts a certain Asur Dadah was found, who was left-handed and well known for his skill in throwing a knife. He is in the service of a famous "boss" of the city underground, a "Sir Winston", with whom Chief Inspector Stross had long since had a score to settle. However, investigations in that direction gave no results and no evidence was found against Asur Dadah.

It should be said here that the notes in the "Blue Book" prove that Chief Inspector Stross did not manage during his lifetime to solve the cases connected to that of Lempytzka & Co, as he called it.

We should also add that two more things connected with this case happened after the death of Eugene Stross. A new board of directors was appointed at the "Plusquam City" Bank after the murder of the chairwoman of the board Lady Hecht, and this new board was presided over by Mr. Ishigumi, a Japanese businessman with a "50 dollar" magical smile. Lempytzka's safe at the "Plusquam City" bank was broken into and another murder took place, in August of 2005. The most guarded man in town was killed then, the aforementioned "Sir Winston". On "Winston's" neck there were twelve bruises from fingers that had choked him. It seemed as though the perpetrator of the crime had seven fingers on one hand. Chief Inspector Stross himself noted in one place in the "Blue Book" that he had seen strange gloves with seven fingers on the left hand and five on the right on Miss Klozewitz. Future in-

vestigations into the death of "Sir Winston" will have to take that into account as well.

The date of "Sir Winston's" death in August of 2005 was predicted in an incredible manner in the notes entered by Chief Inspector Stross into the "Blue Book" during 2003, and so that entire diary note shall be laid out here. Namely, in that place Mr. Eugene Stross wrote down the following words:

Late last night I passed by the inn "The Midnight Sun" and saw Alex Klozewitz with a stud in his eyebrow inside. In front of him there was a glass of red wine. I waved to him and entered, for in our line of work accidental meetings can be the most fruitful.

"What are you drinking?" I asked cordially, and he replied that it was a Hungarian wine, "Buffalo Blood", and ordered me a glass of the same.

Settling on the chicken coop by the bar I glanced into the mirror before us and to my amazement I did not see his image in the form of Miss Sandra with a fan in her hair as I had expected. That day the female side of his androgyne nature was obviously not present. In the mirror I could plainly see only his image with shaven head and a stud in his eyebrow.

"I always forget to ask you something about your work, which I don't really understand very well. The court, of course, ruled that your business activities were, except for one accidental error, faultless, it was established that you pay your taxes regularly, so I'm not asking something to do with the inquest. I'd like to know whether, in your complex activities, you are forced to certain, how shall I put this, conniving, cunning, to certain deceits, or games with dates...?"

"Why certainly!" retorted Klozewitz, "that is unavoidable."

"Well, of what nature is this conniving?"

"Here, let me give you an example. In his dream Distelli, through Pushkin, searched for the devil so the devil could foretell how and when he would die. But no devil is a devil every day. He becomes the devil only on his birthday, which is on the "day of the beast", meaning every 666 days. Before and after that day he does not even recall being a devil... Well, now, for Duchess Marina Sendomirska to be able to prophesy in Distelli's dream how Pushkin would die (meaning Distelli), it was necessary to arrange for Distelli to have that dream the exact day and night when Sendomirska was in "operating condition", namely precisely when she was the devil. Otherwise she would be an ordinary beautiful woman and would understand nothing of what Pushkin and Distelli were asking her, let alone be able to prophesy anything about it. It was also hard to arrange for Duchess Marina Sendomirska to appear in Lempytzka's dream at the very moment when her devilish nature was functional, so that she could prophesy to her double in the dream, Cikindyal, and Lempytzka herself when and how they would die..."

"Fascinating! But how do you come to know all this?" I asked.

"Well I myself, to be honest, don't know all these things every day. Yesterday, for example, I would not have been able to explain it at all, or tomorrow I presume... You just happened to come along today, when I have all this at hand... However today is my birthday, but it has not turned out very happily."

"Congratulations; do tell me what it was that you did not succeed in?"

"Today I failed to settle a score with somebody who has been threatening me for a long time. I usually undertake such settlements on my birthday. But instead of taking care of him I had more important things to do today. And now it's almost midnight and too late for everything this time".

"How does he threaten you?"

"With cutting off a finger."

"Who is it, in the name of the Lord?"

"There's no need for you to concern yourself with it as well, Chief Inspector. I shall have another chance yet to settle that score. I don't like to be threatened anew all the time."

"Are you announcing a murder, Mr. Klozewitz?"

"Yes. I'll even tell you when it will occur."

Klozewitz gazed at the ceiling, counting something on his fingers.

"It will be in exactly 666 days' time, meaning I will kill him sometime in August of 2005."

Then Klozewitz finished off his "Buffalo Blood" and went to the restroom. I rushed after him, because interesting conversations can be continued there as well, and how, for in such places they are not just the usual chats as a rule. When I laid eyes on him, I froze, and he burst into laughter. He was pissing blood and the urinal before him was all sprinkled with red droplets.

At first I thought: why would somebody laugh while pissing blood... unless... it was not his, but "Buffalo Blood"?

And then he peppered me with his gaze and I fled from the inn as fast as my legs would carry me...

Because of this note and several others of that nature, the "Blue Book" of Chief Inspector Stross should be described more closely. The diary is finely bound in blue cloth with gilded letters and the Inspector usually made entries in the evening, sometimes in the small hours with large shadows, but always with his familiar female smile upon his face. Apart from notes and comments about various other cases that the Chief Inspector had investigated during his operating in his field of expertise, which will not concern us here, there are some accidental remarks there as well. For example, on one page there is a picture drawn by the inept hand of the Inspector himself of a landscape with woods and meadows that turned out somewhat like the fleece of a mangy sheep with bits of wool fallen out in places. Right after that the "Blue Book" contains the French translation of a gallant poem "About Beautiful Catherine" whose street was devoid of mud, for all the mud was carried away by her boyfriends on their "heels"... Sometimes these notes and at times already deaf memories can sound strange, even kinky, but if we take into account the fact that Stross did not expect anybody to read them (expect perhaps after his death), everything becomes more understandable. The comments are sometimes quite short, like some kind of saying, or an adage of a person awake alone at night, sometimes they are interrupted in mid-thought, but a man need not don a bow tie to put on his slippers. Here is another entry from Stross's diary chosen at reach:

When I think about it now, I come to the conclusion that I fell prey on several occasions to the trickery of Klozewitz, who presented himself to me face to face as a man, and his reflection in the mirror as a woman. He as so-called Alex, and she as so-called Sandra (a name put together from two parts: Alex(S)andra). Or else they would make an ass of me the other way around, when he, with the stud in his eyebrow, sat in the mirror, and Sandra with her Madonna smile in the pews at the "Symptom House" "temple". And they claimed that it was all due to the fact that they were an "androgyne being". As though they were the only androgyne being in the world and as though the answer to the riddle lay there and not in the mirror.

Therefore I decided to consult on this matter with somebody who could give an impartial judgment on the matter in question. I seeked out Miss Ileana Shimokovich, who works and is officially registered as an "astrologer". I wish I had not. Here is what Miss Shimokovich told me:

"This is no deceit! Whether you see an androgyne creature in both forms, female and male, in person in one, and in the mirror in the other form, depends not on the androgyne but on yourself."

"How so?" I asked, amazed.

"Androgynes in dual form cannot be seen by everybody. To "everybody", whether they are reflected in water, in a mirror or out of it, they are always of the same image. Androgynes can be told apart and their male and female form spotted separately only by those that have evil intentions towards the androgyne being... Such evil-meaning ones gain "Cain's eyesight". And see things in a different way than the rest of us...

Many readers of the "Blue Book" are no doubt wondering how the "Symptom House" came about other people's dreams, and whether and how such transactions could be possible at all. Chief Inspector Stross wondered about this as well and so he wrote down in the "Blue Book" something to do with this matter:

Both Lempytzka and her sister Sophia Androsovich had gurus. Each her own. I visited the guru of Sophia Androsovich and posed to him the question of whether it was possible to acquire other people's dreams like trading goods, the way that "Symptom House" does. The reply was ambiguous:

"I could not say, precisely. I deal in a different field of work. All I know is the following. We usually glimpse from wake into dreams. There are undoubtedly people that can glance the other way, from dreams into wake. If one looks in the right direction, from a dream it might be possible to see other people's dreams. Not just one, but a herd of some person's dreams, all of them. And so perhaps such rare "gurus" or "authorized ones" can load still undreamt dreams into the psyche of a person "prepared" for that. And prepared to pay for such a service. Such "gurus" tell their customers: if you listen carefully, you can hear the future..."

"But how do they come about their goods?"

"They claim: dreams are a particular energy; in fact the accumulated negative karma from previous lives. And more importantly, the future and the past are mingled in dreams, for in dreams there is no present to separate them. If from that world with no present, from dreams, then, you were to take a look at the Universe, at the constellation where the dreamed and undreamt dreams of a person born under the sign being observed are drifting, you would be able to see and read his dreamed and undreamt dreams, for the present, which does not exist there among the stars either, would not get in the way. That is

how traders of dreams come about their goods. Others, yet, say that it is the other way around, that in dreams there is no past, no future, that everything in dreams is one great, eternal present, the same present that fills the Universe. And they conclude the following:

"Even if it is not possible to acquire and sell other people's dreams today, that procedure remains as a possibility and is forthcoming endlessly in the future, so it should be taken into account almost as though it were truly undertaken and existing..."

"So they say. And what do you think of all this?"

"I think that it is all one big "maybe" and in conclusion we could probably laugh at all this and wave it away..."

Unlike the guru, I can neither laugh nor wave it away, for the "Symptom House" company is surrounded by many dead people.

Even more such characteristic notes could be found in Chief Inspector Stross's blue book. Here we shall settle with setting forth one or two more:

Soon after the murder of the betting-shop manager at the hippodrome Isaiah Cruise, I went to pay a visit to his wife. Mrs. Ora lived in a fine house complete with service. A slightly sloppy servant stepped out before us, of the kind described in the proverb "his belt is not threaded through every loop", and placed us in a large parlor. He asked us to wait for madam. We set about looking around us immediately. On a chest with a lot of mosaic woodwork we noticed two silver hands in front of a mirror. There were rings and bracelets slipped on them. As we were looking them over, a thin female voice came from behind our backs:

"Good afternoon. You're examining my silver hands? They were a gift from Isaiah Cruise. Don't look at the nails, I never seem to find the time to varnish them. I don't know if "Revlon" or "Max Factor" would be better? Besides, perhaps they seem all right like this?"

We turned around and saw a girl about 14 years old.

"Dear child, could we see the madam, your mother?"

"Hardly. I don't even remember my mother," replied the girl with a devilish smile, "I am alone here now, since my husband, Isaiah, is deceased as well... I am Madam Ora, but I did not have time to become Ora Cruise. We could not get married for I am not of age yet. But there you have it..."

I need not mention that the matter turned into a failed trip. On the way back to the station my assistant remarked:

"Did you notice anything unusual about those silver hands with the rings?"

"Yes. There was about half a million dollars in jewelry there."

"That's not what I meant. Did you examine the nails on those silver hands?"

"?"

"I looked them over carefully. They look like real human nails removed from all ten fingers of some unfortunate creature... And that coot wants to varnish them!"

Listening to those words I wondered where I had recently noticed fingers without nails on somebody... And I remembered. "Sir Winston", the man of power in the city underground has not a single nail on his fingers. Is it possible that Isaiah Cruise pulled all the nails off his hands?

Finally, permit us to lay forth the following hundred notes made by the late Chief Inspector Eugene Stross in his "Blue Book". These notes are also the promised endings to this novel. Each reader can choose his own end and thus receive a unique item.

MAKE YOUR CHOICE!

♦

1

The night is standing still. As I close my eyes through the dusk the clock is staring at me with all four of its red eyes... The murder at the hippodrome which has not yet been solved is forcing me into insomnia. It was committed in a very unusual way. The murderer shot the victim in the neck from behind. He didn't aim at the head or the body, which are easier to hit, but at the neck. Just as a beast tears at the spine of its victim from behind. My entire investigation on this case seems to me like licking a pot from the outside.

2

In Madam Lempytzka's "dream about footsteps" spirits are invoked in one place. I thought that it might be interesting to consult with somebody skilled in the field of the occult, perhaps even with a spiritualist or some medium. As our lads from the police department frequently visit such dens as well, they asked me: "Where would you like to go about this matter, to Constantinople or to Paris?"

"Paris," I blurted out without giving it much thought. They sent me to some Madame Louvet, and she gave me further directions, in Paris, at the "Places des voges" in the attic of the building next to the "Victor Hugo" museum.

Madame Superville received me in a gleaming dining-room overlooking the royal cavalry monument in the park. She asked me whom I would like to invoke and whether I had any particular question for this person. When I replied that the person's name was Marquezine Androsovich Lempytzka and the question: who is responsible for her death? she sent me on to Monsieur Lenain at the "House of Nicolas Flamel". Lenain invited me for some wine at the inn beneath his abode and there I learned what I was to do if I wished to receive from the late Lempytzka the reply to the question of who was responsible for her death.

We sat in the semidarkness with a candle, wine and "beggars' macaroni". He mentioned matter-of-factly that this semidarkness was one of the oldest dusks in Paris - it was located in the house of the famous alchemist couple, Pernella and Nicolas Flamel, from late Medieval times.

"Man is not made of water, as they usually say, but of thirst," said the little man from the semidarkness, "but there are other important energies present in life as well, such as fear, heat, hunger, pain, and so on. They form something like a forgotten language. Memories of the *deceased are not made of the recollections of physical objects, for they no longer have any idea of what that might be at all, but become recollections of the "energies" that drove them through life. That's why there is this link between the living and the dead. It is the joint non-materialistic build of the ones and the others, and that is why two worlds can touch there - this world and the other. Therefore, write down all your energies on a piece of paper as they come to mind and, without changing the order, mark them with the letters of the alphabet from A to Z. Don't forget love, hatred, joy and sadness, scents and stenches. That will be important for the further procedure...*

He sipped his "Bordeaux" and concluded:

"And now we come to the most important link in the whole story and it will cost you as many tens of euros as you have years."

When I paid him, Monsieur Lenain added:

"What you need to do next and how, that will be revealed to you by somebody else, not I. I have told you as much as can be said here. To continue you must go to Egypt and in the Copt part of the city, near the church there, find Mrs. Zoida, who decorates eyes with Egyptian colors. Everybody there knows her and she is not difficult to reach... By the way, that Zoida had occasion to meet your Lempytzka...

"Nonsense," I thought.

As I parted from Monsieur Lenain I came to the conclusion: I needn't go as far as Egypt to throw my money away. I can do that quite nicely in Paris, or at home.

3

Mr. Erlangen, who was accused of the murder of Madam Lempytzka since he overstepped the measures of necessary self-defense, is now serving a prison sentence. However, he still keeps claiming that he has a witness, a passerby who can confirm that he shot at Lempytzka in self-defense. The name of this witness is supposed to be Erwin, who was walking nearby when he heard shots and came inside in case his help was needed. He was prepared to testify before the court in favor of the accused Erlangen and gave him his phone number 0389-430-23066, dictating it into Erlangen's mobile. However, Erlangen found no Erwin at that number, for it was the number of a kindergarten.

I believe that Erlangen made this witness up.

4

I spoke to Lempytzka on several occasions and I know that she would not be satisfied with the sentences that the court brought forth in "her" case. She would have felt that Klozewitz had "gotten away with it" in court and that he deserved a much more severe sentence. For what?

I'm trying to recollect Lempytzka. But in my memories she is never in motion. She is always still. And I cannot hear her speak. She is not a movie in my memories, not even a silent one, but a collection of snapshots, a sum of still moments that have forever missed their moment. Behind her remained many deceased kisses and even more of those unuttered, unarticulated kisses. And her murderer whom she loved very much.

5

In the court documents related to the death of Lady Hecht it is written that this was a murder committed out of jealousy. The murderer, Madam Lempytzka, and the murdered, Lady Hecht, were both mistresses of the same person - Maurice Erlangen. No wonder. He is a man for whom it is always springtime.

6

Madam Lempytzka killed Lady Hecht with a "Combat 586 Magnum", an extremely expensive killing device for which she never had a license. I discovered later on that the revolver belonged to her late lover Distelli. The late Distelli probably carried that costly weapon more as an ornament, and during the breaking and entering into his apartment that Lempytzka mentioned he did not use it. Perhaps he did not know how.

The same type of revolver was used by Erlangen when he shot Madam Lempytzka. For his "Magnum" type 586 Erlangen possessed an official permit to carry a firearm, and the weapon was listed as the property of the "Plusquam City" bank. Erlangen worked as manager of the high-security deposit box department and he carried a weapon in this capacity.

We might add according to that Latin saying that we had to learn in school: "Habeunt sua fata magni" - firearms have their destiny as well.

7

I visited the pastor of the Russian church who buried Lempytzka. I asked him if he could tell me anything about Lempytzka that would be of assistance in the further investigation. He had two smiles, the left and the right one, he wore his hair woven into a tail and a beautiful cassock with a cross upon the breast. With his left smile he told me:

"As the sky in water passes through its own grave, so the soul in the body passes through our death... And as for your investigation, I will tell you a story that might be able to help."

With his finest right smile he began:

"There is an ancient custom by the Caspian sea. Two men that are in conflict over something go out onto the shore, accompanied by a priest. He says a prayer, the same one every time, and while the prayer lasts they have to resolve their dispute, whether verbally or by wrestling. In any case they have to end the matter by the time the prayer ends, at the latest. Their conflict can be settled before that time, but by no means after the prayer is over. Thus everything must be resolved before the "Amen!",

Anyhow, there was a man who had to battle with his enemy in the described manner several times, both verbally and with his fists. And each time his opponent managed to end the conflict at the moment the prayer was ending, and he always won. The loser came to the priest and asked him for advice, just as you have come to me now. And here is what the priest said to him:

"Your opponent waits for the moment at the end of the prayer when the unholy one is mentioned, and precisely then he wins. Try to defeat him before he gets the opportunity for the unholy one to help him..."

8

Erlangen's prison sentence was not pronounced without grounds. His claim of shooting in self-defense is not in accordance with the truth, for the ballistics reports showed that Madam Lempytzka had fired all three of the bullets that had been in her "Magnum" at Lady Hecht. At the moment when Erlangen stepped into the room and drew his weapon to kill Lempytzka, she could not have been intending to shoot, nor could she have fired at him, since her revolver was already empty. In her revolver there had been no seventh bullet.

9

"Who taught you to catch other people's dreams like a cat catching mice?"

"Some people inherit this gift. Actually rachitic memories, lame thoughts, thoroughbred kisses and cracked loves are inherited, or forgetfulness for names, and so what you are inquiring about is inherited as well. But the skill of catching another's dream we did not inherit. I shall tell you how we learned this, and you can judge for yourself. The essence of it is a trick with time. Here's how it all began.

We had a cat with greenish stripes. It was an ordinary cat, just like any other, and like all others it hunted in the garden and in attics and basements. Her name was Maxima. One morning she brought a slightly larger animal into the garden between her teeth. It seemed like a rat. We could see that it was a youngster, but could not recognize what it was. From *a distance that caught animal looked like a newly born rabbit, or some such creature. We were horrified to think for a moment that the cat had brought a tiny baby from somewhere, but we saw straight away that this was not the case.*

However, Maxima brought her catch and dropped it in front of the stairs. Then we grabbed the captured little beast by the tail, lifted it up and got a good look at it. It really was a youngster, but not a rabbit. It had hairy legs with tiny hoofs, but its upper ones had little paws with five fingers and sharp claws. It wore a beard and through the fur on its head we could see two tiny horns, and two pointy ears were protruding. It also had a tail that we were holding it by before we dropped it onto the ground. We thought that it was dead, that the cat had strangled it in fact, but she poked it with her paw to play a bit and it moved. It opened first one and then the other eye and out came a tongue with a hole in the middle. The cat continued to play with it, but she showed no intention of eating it. To the contrary, she picked it up and put it in her basket as though it were her kitten, licked it, making its auburn hair gleam and the tiny animal fell asleep.

In the morning, during breakfast, the cat circled around the table as usual. At one moment, to our astonishment, she leapt up onto a chair, sat down and said quite clearly:

"Please, some more milk..."

"You can talk?" I asked her in a quivering voice. We, of course, knew what was to come, that is why we took in a cat with greenish stripes. She replied in German:

"I speak when I must," averting her gaze towards the little animal whose tail had just fallen off. It brought it and showed it to the cat, and the cat was frightened and

hissed. Then the little beast laughed at which its ears spread wide, and the cat laughed as well, though unwillingly. As opposed to the cat, the youngster was quite mute. But it forced the cat to speak and she did so obediently like a conveyor belt for words, horrified of herself.

In the evening the cat came to sit in our laps and purr as usual. Her purring suddenly turned into irregular French verbs and nouns and finally she said, looking above our heads:

"Yellow stars twinkle more slowly than white ones, because yellow travels more slowly through the Universe. Their lights pass through all seven Heavens, some of which rotate swiftly, some more slowly. And you need to know how to see all that and locate what is where..."

Then she showed us how other people's dreams can be caught among the stars. We soon started catching them like mice... It's not at all difficult, like the alchemist Flamel said of making gold: "Now my wife Pernella, too, can make gold whenever she desires..."

First we caught dreams here, on Earth, all around us, still alive while they were dreamt. And then we caught dreamt and undreamed dreams from all seven of the Heavens. Those dreams there are all that remains of a mortal after his death, like the hair or feces of a cat remain when a cat dies after spending all seven of its lives.

In the meanwhile the little animal disappeared, and the cat stopped talking...

In conclusion I might say that we knew in advance that such a thing could happen to us with a striped cat, but it could also not have happened.

"Is there no easier way to catch dreams than that horrible business with the cat?"

"Of course there is."
"?"
"You need to learn how to dream other people's dreams instead of your own. And thus matters are solved."
"Would you like to hear my opinion on all that?"
"Speak up. Why not. It amounts to the same anyway."
"I think that none of what you told me is the truth."
"You know what, truth is like a vitamin. Maybe you'll need it, and maybe you won't."

10

I visited the grave of Madam Lempytzka on All Souls' Day. I wanted to see if anybody else would come. And who came. Nobody. Yet she had tits one of which was worth a thousand dollars, and the other nothing, for who pays for one gets the other for free. She could have kneaded bread with those breasts, like a song says.

11

Retired maritime captain Ilija Skud lives near the Erlangen villa and I visited him for tea and a chat. In front of the captain's house there was a bench, and on the bench nine cats. It looked like the seat was lined with fur. The tea turned into peppered rum, and the chat into the following muddle:

"Did you see anyone enter the Erlangen villa on the mentioned date?"

"Yes. Two ladies. They didn't enter together."
"What did they look like?"
"The one that went in first had an a la tramontana hairstyle."
"What does that mean?"
"I can see that you're not a sailor, Mr. Inspector. You see, when a "tramontana" is blowing the waves are particularly curly. The lady that entered the villa first had just such curly waves of hair."
"And the other one?"
"The other one came much later. She wore a "bonaza" hairdo... But you don't know that either. "Bonaza" is "calm sea"."
"And did you, captain, sir, notice any men enter the villa at that time?"
"Dear Mr. Inspector, I usually pay no attention to men and they can peacefully walk in and out right past me as much as they please, to me it's as if they're not there. I only have eyes for women. Besides, one should never talk about men with the police. That always smacks you in the nose... Anyway, the two men didn't go inside together, either."
"And that's all?"
"By no means. Surely you would not refuse another glass of Cuban rum?"

I left astounded. Erlangen, then, was telling the truth, a witness to the murder did appear in the villa but could not be located afterwards. A witness whose name Erlangen claims to be Erwin.

Who is Erwin? And do I know him without even being aware of it?

12

During an inquest concerning the murder of Isaiah Cruise, Mr. Ishigumi, called "the 50 dollar smile", told me in confidence that, immediately after the murder, a woman took the elevator to the 4th floor of the hippodrome building, where the murder was committed. The fourth floor, where the working premises of Isaiah Cruise are, can only be accessed by means of a special key that, as it seemed, only Cruise possessed.

Who that woman was in the "red blouse and jeans", as Mr. Ishigumi recollected, has not been established to date. Why did she go there? Did she meet the murderer? Did she know that a murder was being prepared and that it had already been committed? Did she wish to convince herself that Cruise had been killed? Where did she get the key from? Was she Mrs. Ora, the wife of Isaiah Cruise? Did she not, perhaps, engage a paid assassin? In that case, was it a murder out of jealousy and amorous revenge? Finally, did Mr. Ishigumi recognize her, but decide to keep quiet about it for some reason?

13

Think of a beautiful woman,

Double her beauty,

Triple it.

Raise it to the square.

And forget her.

That is Lempytzka.

14

That business with the selling of the future and the selling of dreams should not be completely legal. But, as an astrologer, Mr. Alexander Klozewitz had documents that were quite in order, he paid his taxes regularly, his business activities were registered and there was nothing that could be done apart from (as we in the police force would say) "charging a fine for spitting in public". And that was done. If his customers had stated that they had been deceived by him, that would have been quite a different matter. As it is, there remains a question-mark that I place in this book in green ink and I comfort myself with the saying that the path towards a hit leads through many misses.

15

I informed myself with an expert in Slavic languages and literature about the verses by Pushkin which the late Distelli had dreamt. Those verses really do exist in Pushkin's opus. However, in that version of the dream recorded for us by Klozewitz, Distelli did not dream them in Russian, but in some other language, so they seem as thought they were translated or listened to like several beats of music. The expert in Slavic languages had another interesting observation as well. The three segments of the dream in which Pushkin sits in a carriage and drives home correspond to the verses from Pushkin's poem entitled "The Coach of Life". As though the people from Pushkin's poetry had risen, sat in the chaise with the coachman and driven off towards their death in Distelli's dream.

16

It is interesting to note that the great boss of the underground, "Sir Winston" or the man with the cigar, who always knows in advance who would be killed in town, had no idea about the murders in the Erlangen villa. Although we are constantly on his tail, not even the slightest connection could be spotted between "Sir Winston" and the murderers in that shooting, which are, as the court determined, Madam Lempytzka and Mr. Erlangen. The man with the cigar did not dip his fingers into that matter. Those fingers of his without nails.

17

"Our thoughts are just the building material with which we construct a house around ourselves to protect us and separate us from the world. It is unfortunate that they cannot do so, for they are soft and flexible and not intended for this. What the purpose of thoughts is we have not yet determined..." (Lempytzka in a conversation with her guru Zdenyikin.)

When I asked Zdenyikin what he thought of Lempytzka, he told me:

"At times she was able to see everything around her in the way that angels see this world."

"?"

As though she had one eye deeper, and the other shallower. In one she carried the day, in the other the night, she saw the left side as the right, and the right as the right, always taking ratios into consideration: how much water there was on Earth in comparison to land (3:1), how much water there was inside of her compared to her beautiful body (3:1), and how much Sky there was compared to the firm ground of the stars, taking the ratio 3:1 into consideration here as well. In short, she looked like somebody whose nails had stopped growing long ago.

18

I noticed in the report on dreams submitted by Alexander Klozewitz that one of the characters moved from one dream to the other, appeared and operated in both dreams, both in the dream of Madam Lempytzka and that of Mr. Distelli. It was the demoness from the dream on the death of Pushkin, Duchess Marina Mnishek Sendomirska, who prophesied to both Pushkin and Distelli at the same time that they would die of an injury to the stomach. She moved into Lempytzka's dream as well and foretold the death of the boy in the dream, whom Lempytzka turned into as soon as she fell asleep. She foretold him a double, true androgyne death which came true completely. She told Cikindyal, the boy from Lempytzka's dream at the time when he was already grown-up, the following:

"You shall die of a firearm twice, but once in a dream and as a man, and the second time in your waking hours, as a woman!"

This prophesy by Duchess Sendomirska came true literally as well. Major Cikindyal in Lempytzka's dream died somewhere on the war front, but had two graves. Both graves were in Lempytzka's dream. While the killed Cikindyal was buried in the second grave, the first re-

mained empty as though waiting for the death of Lempytzka which was foretold would be female and during her waking hours, the death at the hand of Erlangen.

19

When I sent Klozewitz a request to submit an official report on the dreams of Distelli and Lempytzka, he objected at first claiming that he was not a psychiatrist and that it was not a part of his profession to describe and analyze dreams. When I drew his attention to the fact that he possessed tapes with the descriptions of these dreams, he added that those tapes were not worth much and that he considered the describing of dreams to be a futile effort:

"Dreams cannot be led by the reins like one can lead a mule in a straight line. And when a dream is recanted, it must be pulled by the reins just so, straight forward. Therefore the court will have to accept and take into account the inevitable ineptness of my report arising from the stringing together of the clustered and dispersed dreams of Distelli and Lempytzka in order to slip their dreams through the needle-eye of sentences, the words of which are always a caravan of ganders flying South one behind the other..."

20

It is interesting that three very prominent murders in town this year were committed with the same rare and expensive type of revolver. This was a "Combat Magnum" 586, used during the murder of: Isaiah Cruise, manager of the hippodrome betting-shop, then during the murder of Lady Hecht and almost simultaneously during the murder of Lempytzka. They were held by three hands. Two are known to me - those are Lempytzka and Erlangen, but I do not know who the third was, the murderer at the hippodrome.

21

I did not inform Madam Lempytzka during our visit to the "Symptom House" that I went to the mortuary several days before the funeral of her lover, Mr. Distelli, and saw him there. I might add that such visits are part of a routine in my job and that I have plenty of experience with coronary work of all kinds.

Even for a deceased he looked very poorly and it was obvious that he would not go very long or far on the other side of the grave either. It was also obvious that he had long since dreamt his death clearly and personally, but had not noticed it lost in the dream. And so it leapt out at him from an unexpected angle. Namely, on the basis of the segments of his dreams from the future that Klozewitz had sold him he had expected to die of a stomach wound, and so he hoped that the matter with the cancer of the esophagus he was suffering from was curable. It was not until metastases appeared on his stomach that he realized that it was the end. And precisely the end that the dreams on Pushkin had prophesied.

What does metastasis mean in my case? Should I also perform some kind of metastasis in my investigation, and transfer the focal point from the investigation so far onto some other area in fact? Seek for some other culprits instead of the ones that I have been persecuting until now?

22

I went to visit Erlangen. After a brief greeting I showed him the purple scarf from Lempytzka's safety deposit box and asked him if he recognized the object.

"No," he said, "whose is it?"

"I found it in Lempytzka's safe. In the safe at your bank."

Then Erlangen did something that I had not done, although I should have. He smelled the scarf and said:

"Hugo Boss" - that is a male scent and cannot be Lempytzka's, but beneath that scent there is another, unavoidable one," and handed me the scarf.

As soon as I sniffed it I realized that it bore the stench of grease for oiling weapons. And so we now know what was lying in the purple scarf from the safety deposit box of Madam Lempytzka. Distelli's "Combat Magnum" lay wrapped in that scarf in the safe at the "Plusquam City" bank. In other words, in the bank run by Lady Hecht lay the revolver with which she was to be killed. But we can go no further from there. That after Distelli's death Lempytzka had his revolver we had already been quite familiar with, so this discovery holds no water either.

You always come up against a wall. A wall of lament, a wall of silence, or a wall of stone. But there is no wall when you need one to protect your back from a knife.

23

During a visit to the "Symptom House" company I asked Miss Sandra Klozewitz whether other people's dreams could be bought from her as well, but the undreamt ones, meaning other people's dreams from the future. You wish, for example, to know what the person you are interested in will dream in three years' time.

"That would be a form of spying on somebody else's future."

"Precisely," I retorted.

"I think that it could be done, but there is a certain difficulty involved. The difficulty lies not in the sum of money, which is negligible for such a service - only 1000 dollars, but in the other conditions that are very hard in such cases, and so I would not recommend that you enter into such a matter."

"Do you believe I would not be able to fulfill them?"

"I believe that you would not wish to fulfill such conditions."

"Did Distelli and Lempytzka fulfill certain conditions that I would not accept?"

"You see, dear Mr. Chief Inspector, they did not request, like yourself, to see other people's future through their dreams, but their own. And see it they did."

24

Rains are pouring down tonight. Water from all centuries is falling to the earth. Literally. And seeping to the bone. Why could dreams of all centuries not tumble down upon us and seep through to our bones? They also circle and flow like water. Perhaps Klozewitz is not such a quack as I believe and as Lempytzka used to say, although she abandoned such thoughts. Besides, why should everybody think the same in order for something to become the truth? If my dreams from the future do not show themselves to me, it's nobody's fault but my own. Does that mean that they do not show themselves to others? If you cry, does that mean the bicycle you are riding on is crying as well?

25

A cage, and inside it a large flower the color of saffron. A few scented pillows filled with sweet basil and an Indian device in the window which I was told was a wind-trap, something like a mouse-trap for monsoons. Finally, in the bedroom a real, true Venetian gondola instead of a bed. Suspended by chains from the ceiling it hung there, all in black lacquer.

These are the things I noticed when I searched the apartment of Madam Lempytzka. And something else. On the wall of the room a drawing of Lempytzka's with many notes around it and the following writing above the drawing:

THE BALL OF TIME

"Time is like the soul," wrote Lempytzka on that wall, "it has its auras in the form of balls which are contained one in the other and at the bottom it holds (as the Universe holds the Earth) its heavy body.

The outer aromatic and transparent layer in the Ball of Time is eternity. It is connected by light to God, and by one bar of music to the future, which it holds beneath *itself as the next, lower layer, or layer inside the Ball of Time. That layer-future is also transparent. Beneath it is a see-through layer of the deepest, unhistorical past: it is the unhistorical body of time and it touches the most distant future just as East and West touch upon this Earth. Under this layer is a nontransparent one containing the historical past, or historical time. At the bottom of the Ball of Time is the hard personal time of our lives, the nontransparent core of the present, that which our clocks measure and lose."*

In the middle of the drawing of the Ball of Time Lempytzka glued her "Chopard" wristwatch to the wall, stopping it at the time of death of her lover Distelli and never wearing it again.

26

Deep autumn, and within it even deeper night. Around me the human race is tearing apart one of its freshly born days - hour by hour... In such moment there is no wisdom in this world. Only hunches, intuitions, instincts, dreams and hatreds function.

If in that plane I question myself about the Lempytzka case it amounts to the following: Erlangen is less guilty than could be concluded from the sentence he received. Distelli is more guilty than he seems, and than can be proven. Lempytzka had to have somebody else behind her as well, but we don't know whom. Klozewitz is the most suspicious of them all, but there is almost no tangible argument against him. Of him nothing can be proven apart from the small financial violation that he already paid for, laughing with that fake moustache of his.

27

Since three murders (those of Isaiah Cruise, the betting-shop manager at the hippodrome, Lady Hecht and Lempytzka) were committed with the same, rare type of weapon "Combat Magnum" 586, I requested the ballistics experts to check out and compare the bullets with the revolvers. We were lacking one of the revolvers at that (the one that Isaiah Cruise had been killed with), while all of the bullets removed from the three aforementioned bodies were at our disposal.

And I was right to request such a report. I have foretelling pockets filled with the future in which I turn my keys until something clever comes to mind. Namely, Isaiah Cruise was also killed with Distelli's revolver and at a time when Distelli was already lying in hospital with a metastasis that he was to die of. Who had been in possession of his revolver at that time? If Lempytzka had it, she had no motive: why would she kill the hippodrome betting-shop manager whom she had probably not even known? Besides, Miss Androsovich claimed that Marquezine Lempytzka, her sister, had spent the entire evening with her, that she had been crying over her lover's illness and that they had comforted each other and gone to bed together.

28

I found a coin on the sidewalk today. It was gleaming and I stooped down and picked it up. It means luck, or so they say. A lady passing by paused and asked me:

"Are you sure that what you have just done is safe?"

"Could this be dangerous?" I asked in surprise and she retorted, shaking her head:

"Perhaps the coin is not its own."

"?"

"You don't know what that means? Well, let me tell you. The coin might have a purpose. This precise one. It might be some kind of unique item.

"?"

"Perhaps somebody tried to remove a spell from himself, and in order to remove it cast it upon the coin, and the coin onto the ground, expecting somebody to pick it up in greed. And so spells are passed on, to somebody else, and in this case that would be you..."

I left, astounded. So the spell-casting with coins of Count Ragusinsky in Distelli's dream was not invented. It exists to this day. Therefore Pushkin also knew about this, if the dreams of the deceased are to be believed, and I am to learn of this in the street...

29

There is good reason to believe that Klozewitz and his trading of dreams is in fact just a plain fraud, a trick and charlatanry, as Lempytzka called it. It can further be assumed that both of the writings that he presented to the court as a report on the acclaimed dreams of Distelli and Lempytzka were made up by him word for word. For, who is to guarantee that they did indeed dream those dreams?

However, if this is the case, then why did Lempytzka take part in a deal concerning the purchase of dreams *from her own future with Klozewitz even though she knew that the entire "Symptom House" was a fraud and charlatanry? Perhaps for the very reason that she gave me the first day - to disclose Klozewitz, and discover the manner in which Klozewitz was connected to her lover's death and in which measure and respect he was responsible for it. Perhaps on this path and for these reasons she died? Stepped in deeper somewhere than was permitted?*

30

How I wish I were not an inspector, but a smelter, that I had a workshop for bells in 1854 on the other side of the river of Paradise, near Karamata's house from the 18th century. I would drink wine from the finest bell, from one of my ears a willow would grow, from the other grapes and you would all be but a pain in the iron rooster on the foundry roof to me...

31

The dream is wiser than the dreamer and much, much older. Still, I have never been particularly interested in dreams. I believe that dreams are the excrements of our fears. In any event there are six customary holiday dreams in the life of a man and just as many dreams for workdays. And that is all.

But, my job requires sacrifice, so when I drifted into this muddle with Klozewitz and everything that the "Symptom House" sells, I began reading Jung. He says that the dream is a two-pronged tooth or a double-horned *specter, and I that the dream is a three-tailed beast. At least as far as Lempytzka's dream is concerned. If it is true that dreams mean the fulfillment of wishes and that they go even further, and compensate for what we lack in life or have too much of, then we have three compensations with Lempytzka's dream:*

A. The fact that in the androgyne "tail" of the dream Lempytzka turns into a boy and later on identifies with him when he is a grown lad without love affairs, except for one, a lad that women do not like (including his own mother) - all those are the covert and unfulfilled wishes of a sex-bomb such as Lempytzka obviously became very early on. Her fear of her so expressed femininity to which her entire surroundings reacted so aggressively, was compensated by Lempytzka turning into a boy in her sleep, one with no sexual power as yet and horrified of a slightly older, pushy girl.

B. In the female "tail" (branch) of her dream one can plainly see the yearning for a child, which Lempytzka does not have but wishes for.

C. I have not yet studied the "third tail", the male branch in Lempytzka's dream, sufficiently, yet it is the most important one for my inquest procedure, since it is related to the murders. It surpasses my knowledge in this field, and besides it is windy outside, the curtain in my room is pregnant and it is time neither for wake nor for sleep. You should take a book and turn off the light before you open it.

32

I *met Asur Dadah, the man with the 30 dollar smile who works for "Sir Winston", in a casino yesterday and asked him whether he knew anything about the murder at the* hippodrome. Although he had already "done time" and figured that I "held him in my fist", instead of replying he sang me a rap song:

"Ihadaplateoffishearsforsupperlastnightandtheforks- ingsandstingslikeawasp...IwasabouttoslicewhenInoticed- myhandshadchanged...liketwoscaldedgeeseheads- theyeachprotrudedfromtheirsleevesandcouldnotswal- lowtheknifeandfork..."

33

Why was Distelli so occupied by Pushkin, and his work "Boris Godunoff" in particular? In that dream of Pushkin's death that predicts the death of Distelli as well, could there be something more? Why "Boris Godunoff"? Of course, Distelli sang the lead role in the opera by Mussorgsky, but Distelli himself told Madam Lempytzka (and she confided this in me): "I don't like that role, I sing it unwillingly!" Who, then, was Boris Godunoff? A murderer. Apart from others that of prince Dimitri as well. Distelli seems to say: I don't want to become a murderer as well! What is this crime that he was objecting to commit? What crime of his did Distelli wish to avoid when his dream saw Pushkin's entire play as the summoning of the devil and evil spirits, requesting of them in his dream to tell him how to save himself from the "band that was tightening around him"?

What was this band in Distelli's case? The "Symptom House"? Was Distelli being forced by something onto the path of crime and murder? And did he resist, or give in under the pressure despite the wisdom of the dream that was cautioning him against it? He probably *never had the time (even if he had the intention, whatever that intention might have been). He died before that. Or did Distelli flee into illness and death from the murder that he was supposed to commit for some reason, which is not a rare case.*

34

I met Lady Hecht at a reception celebrating the tenth anniversary of her bank. She was with one of the bank officials, a handsome green-eyed man whose name I later learned was Maurice Erlangen.

It was snowing. Each carrying a glass, they retired from the crowd and sat in the artificially heated swing on the tree-covered roof of their building. He was drinking "Chivas", she "Martini". They did not notice me. She seemed frightened, though the reason of the fear could not be determined. I caught a fragment of what she was saying to him. She was obviously under the influence of alcohol:

"Do you know how many have gone to sleep under my hair so far? You don't? Neither do I. And that's not the point. You yourself shall forget soon. But look, it's starting to snow... When the end comes and you pull away from love you'll see how you will smoke from my heat and how snowflakes melt upon you... One does not forget that..."

35

A reputable psychiatrist whose advice I sought concerning the "masculine tail", namely that part of Lempytzka's dream where she turns into an officer and *finds herself in the midst of war, gave the following interpretation. To him it was a compensatory process. In that part of the dream, though in war and the rank of a higher officer, Major Cikindyal, meaning Lempytzka, is completely disinterested in the wartime enterprises of her unit and still occupied by her civilian professional and scientific work. In his opinion the dream in this place is cautioning Lempytzka: "Do not kill!", that is fulfillment in the dream of the desire that Lempytzka does not understand while she is awake, and so she kills her rival in the love triangle, Lady Hecht. In short, Madam Lempytzka's dream, which sees better and broader than she does, is correcting the one-sided and erroneous urges that she has during her waking hours when she isn't listening to her dream, which ended in doom.*

36

A chief inspector with his delicate search for homicidal felonies resembles a man who must step only from one to another fallen leaf... When there is no leaf within reach, he stands and waits for autumn and his step to fall from the sky. It is so with the Distelli-Lempytzka case as well. It seems to me that I am still waiting for autumn...

37

I obtained a warrant to open the safety deposit box held by Lempytzka at the "Plusquam City" bank. Inside it I found only a purple scarf and a piece of paper. Some verses were written out on the paper, obviously dedicated to Lempytzka. Although they were signed by Distelli, I don't know if they were his, or if he copied them down for Lempytzka, for they seem to speak of the age difference between the two of them:

Oh, young lady, bearing time without clock
A timeless watch in my pocket growls
Our names are like hats: when wind howls
Without us remain hats by the flock.

Love so different than yours an ancestor knows,
And you had to teach me to love like a youth;
That another's was easy we both thought the truth,
You'll scarcely manage to learn from the close.

38

I checked with the largest insurance agency in town "Atlas" whether there was a policy on Isaiah Cruise's life. There was, and for a huge sum that had not been paid out, for nobody had applied to collect the money. The sum was to be paid, in case of the insured man's death, to his wife. Was madam Ora, the unwed wife of Isaiah Cruise, hoping for this payment and was that her reason to hire a paid assassin? That is a assumption hard to sustain, for three reasons:

1. Since they were not married she could not legally be presumed to be Isaiah Cruise's wife.
2. Since she was not of age, she could not dispose of that property of her own accord in the near future.

3. Even without the insurance money she is still fabulously rich.

The story with madam Ora always amounts to the same as the Lempytzka case: neither take it nor leave it. And I can continue giving names to the clouds.

39

Although the Lempytzka-Hecht-Erlangen case was legally closed, I cannot escape the feeling that none of it is solved and none of it clear. I am uncertain in particular of whether there is any connection between this case and the murder of Isaiah Cruise at the hippodrome, which was committed with Distelli's "Magnum" at the time when he was in hospital, dying of cancer. Maybe I should start from the beginning, from the witnesses this time. Who are the witnesses in this case? Lempytzka's sister, for example, Miss Sophia Androsovich, whom we overlooked almost entirely. When I called her, she laughed and said into the receiver:

"You've finally thought of me, Mr. Chief Inspector! I was wondering if you would, and when. But we shall not have this conversation in the usual way. I shall not invite you to visit me, for my address is in a sleeping carriage. I love to travel. You will take me out to dinner at one of the better inns, your department pays for such matters anyway."

I did so immediately. As soon as we sat down I asked:

"Did your sister, Madam Lempytzka, kill the hippodrome betting-shop manager, Mr. Isaiah Cruise?"

"What has gotten into you, you handsome man," Miss Androsovich switched to a familiar manner in a flash, "my sister is deceased, there's no need for me to protect her, for there's nothing more that you can do to her, but still let me tell you how it was. At the time when that Cruise of yours was killed and when the news report was broadcast on television, Lempytzka was at my place. She spent the entire evening crying over her singer, who was lying in hospital. Tears made her eyes freckled like a snake's. And as for you, do you want me to tell you what I think of you?

At the age of twenty men are still babies, at thirty they are children, they reach puberty at the age of forty, and after that they're of no serious use any more."

40

I visited the "Symptom House" yesterday and found Alex Klozewitz there. I hadn't seen him since the day he appeared in the courtroom and I wished to speak with him. Since he had settled all the obligations ordered by the court, I felt that my visit would not be too upsetting for him. In the entire Distelli-Lempytzka-Hecht case Klozewitz is the one who has remained the most unclear to me, and I wanted to get another sniff at his "temple". I called him up and announced my visit.

"It would be best if you came in the evening. I believe the weather will be clear," he observed.

That evening he was polite, but "with one hand always behind his back", as we say. I told him that I was interested in his procedure with dreams and asked him to show me something related to my own dreams. The *dreamed or the undreamt ones. He livened up a little and showed me the starry sky from one of the terraces of his dwelling.*

"Which sign was the Chief Inspector born under?" he asked me. When I said that it was "Pisces" he stretched his finger towards the sky and started explaining and pointing out to me:

"In the timeless zone of your constellation, where your dreamed and still undreamt dreams flock, there are four fish. Two of them are, shall we say, "on dry land", while the other two fish are in the region of the "Milky Way". Do you see them? That's where your dreams are drifting. Even those that you are to dream, but will not be able to do so to the end, for some of them will be cut short by your death before they are finished."

"Are you threatening me, Mr. Klozewitz?"

"There's no reason for that. There are many people whose dreams were interrupted by death and there are always plenty of not completely dreamt dreams in the Universe, just as there are not completely read books here... I simply read all this from the stars. Tons of dreams remain without their dreamers every night."

41

The other day I went to see dr. Arnold Macintosh, the late Lempytzka's physician. We sat down to talk about her, or rather I listened carefully without asking any questions. He had moustaches like a bowtie under his nose. He talked about everything else rather than her medical condition.

"Madam Lempytzka loved water. She drank only "Perrier" and the Greek water "Lutraki". She visited various spas looking for a good one throughout northern Africa. Apart from her water cult, she nurtured other characteristics as well. She loved to eat algae and shells, and rare stones were a particular passion of hers. Minerals, crystals, stalactites. I don't know if she had a collection, but she was quite familiar with the matter, she bought a Chinese manual from the 12th century: "Catalogue of Stones", and showed me a ring with a green jasper stone which she believed could "see the future". "Stones are so old that they undoubtedly see further than we do in both directions," she remarked on one occasion..."

Taking my leave from Lempytzka's physician I noticed that his eyes secreted glassy pebbles.

42

Since Erlangen was released from prison on parole, for his behavior in jail had been exemplary, I paid him a visit. To him the visit was not a pleasant one, but he didn't want that to be seen. Besides, people can be grouped into talented hosts and talented guests. Erlangen obviously belonged to the latter group. We had a drink, I asked him if he played the piano standing in the corner of the room, and he raised the lid of the instrument, sat at it and to my astonishment it turned out that the piano did not have tones, but the recorded soundings of all the letters of the alphabet. And in several registers at that - as though they were pronounced by a woman, an old man, a child, a deep male voice, etc. In short, it was a piano that spoke instead of playing. Turning away from this nonsense I asked Erlangen:

"Can you tell me how Madam Lempytzka came to be in the possession of Distelli's revolver?"

Instead of a reply he rattled off the following on the talking piano:

"You are fear risen onto its hind legs, growing sideburns and a beard. Dusk thrives in the paths of your eyes, and laughter among your teeth, but you find it harder and harder to remember. You bear your soul in your nose yet they teach you to sneeze..."

43

Tonight in this diary I will return once more to the question of witnesses in the case of Marquezine Lempytzka. I met (as I have noted here somewhere already) with Miss Androsovich, the late Lempytzka's sister, in an inn. Miss Androsovich appeared on high heels resembling two upside-down Eiffel towers and ordered a carp on honey.

"Did your sister like races?" I began my attack immediately.

"She did. Even as girls we raced which one of us would orgasm first. Marquezine, whose surname wasn't Lempytzka yet then, was quicker and afterwards she was able to orgasm seven times in a row on the same man. She never got her period, I suppose that's why she never had children. Instead of into puberty she rushed straight into menopause... As girls we lived in Vienna. One day she took one of the boys from the neighborhood to the cemetery and taught him how to take her virginity there, in the bell tower. She called it her mystical wedding. In *school, during class, I fondled the student beside me with my left hand beneath the desk, while I solved mathematical equations on the desk with my right. It was no use. While I was doing that to him he was looking at Marquezine, who sat in the desk next to us. Everybody looked at her. The whole school jerked off at my sister, including the teachers, even some of the female ones as well. See, even you want to talk only about Lempytzka, even though I am the one you've taken out to dinner..."*

"But, dear Miss Androsovich, I only meant to use this occasion as well to give you my condolences concerning your sister's death, and that question about horse races was just a matter-of-fact one, like chatting over a meal..."

"She didn't like races. Distelli took her to them. He suited her because he was already aged and didn't jump on top of her twice a day like her first husband did... Although they did go more frequently to dog races. She liked to mate with Distelli's hound. She was the one who taught him one evening when Distelli couldn't, and she wanted it. Distelli watched them and was able to afterwards as well... But, believe me, the myth of Marquezine as a sex bomb is invented and blown out of proportion. Every second woman is a sex bomb. Men who have been both with me and with Marquezine claim that there is hardly any difference in bed and that I am even better in a certain phase... But we shall leave that for the Chief Inspector to conclude for himself, although I believe that you didn't sleep with Lempytzka. Isn't that true?...

I learned only one single thing from my sister."

"?"

"She taught me a verse worth paying for in gold."

"?"

"I won't reveal it to you for now. When you say that verse aloud the tongue movements are such that during oral pleasuring of a woman they cause her to climax."

44

The murder at the hippodrome seems to have fallen during the investigation into the shadow of the double homicide at the Erlangen villa. During the search of the apartment of the late Isaiah Cruise, the hippodrome bettingshop manager, we found out that his wife lives separately in her own house, and that Cruise stayed in both places in turn, in his own apartment and in his wife's house.

His apartment consisted of ordinary bachelor quarters and in it we found only two interesting things. A black male fan from Korea and a slim brass ladies' pipe upon which a metal butterfly had alighted. These two things seemed like they didn't belong to Cruise at all, or to his dwelling. Or they might have belonged to some period in his life which was unbeknownst to us. Was he in the Korean war? With whom? Perhaps with somebody who decided to settle the score with Cruise now.

45

After the visit I paid to Klozewitz the other night the "Symptom House" sent me a gift: an Indian "map" of the sky with the constellation in which my dreams are located, intermingled with billions of other ancient and future dreams from the region of "Pisces".

The map shows the "Milky Way" and within it one of the four fish from my sign of the zodiac. An arrow was shot towards that fish or the two birds above it, but it hit nothing and was probably destined to eternally fly over the fish. Between that one and the second fish of my sign there were two male and one female figure. The female figure was young, with pretty, bare breasts over which she was holding a sunshade. In short white trousers of light Indian fabric she was sitting with crossed legs that looked like two finely sculpted instruments. The man beside her had arms spread wide and the second fish of my sign was passing beneath his right one. That man was wearing a yellow hiton, he had an artificial mole on his forehead and wore red socks. There was a chain tied around his waist that hung down in front and forked so that it bound his feet as well. The two remaining fish of my sign were truly on "dry land" - far from the "Milky Way".

On the other side of the girl beneath the sunshade (which protected her from the overly bright sparkle of the stars, so it might be better to call it a "starshade") stood a man in purple wearing a cap and a black plume. With his left hand he was touching the huge snake that had stretched out its head, looking into the next constellation, at a man picking stars and placing them into a net similar to the kind for catching butterflies. There were already eight stars inside it, and the man was picking the ninth.

Klozewitz's note that accompanied the map of the sky bore the following words:

"This is what the dwelling of your dreams looks like."

Three figures: two men and a woman! Just like in my Distelli-Cruise-Lempytzka investigation. And somebody picking stars. Or perhaps dreams?

46

Tonight I neither feel like sleeping nor like writing in this damn book. The ink is drying, my soul is lost, perhaps it's off skiing somewhere, while I hold my painful feet in a basin of salted wine. I'm lying at the bottom of my thoughts like on the bottom of the beautiful blue Danube. And I look on with horror as the ring on the hand of Miss Sophia Androsovich who is sleeping in my bed twists on her finger, revolving of its own accord.

47

When I turned later on to the question of witnesses in the Lempytzka case, I did so because their taking into consideration during the investigation was quite sloppy. Klozewitz, for example. That's why I decided to go to the "Symptom House" once more. I was greeted by Miss Sandra in the "temple". I didn't manage to get a look at her in the mirror, but I was under the impression that the shaven head and eyebrow with a stud belonging to Alex Klozewitz passed through the mirror during our conversation. Defenseless before Sandra's innocent gaze and navy-blue hair clipped beneath her chin with a cameo as though it were a scarf, I mechanically asked the question that interested me the most:

"Do you like races?"

"Yes. I like Formula 1."

She was cooling herself with a fan sprinkled with stars from the constellation "Cancer".

"That's not what I meant. I meant horse races."

"Not really. I went to the hippodrome once or twice, and once to the dog track. But that doesn't appeal to me. Why do you ask?"

"But, Miss Sandra, I only ask matter-of-factly. I actually came to see you on a business matter. What would your "Symptom House" have to offer me from the assortment at its disposal?"

"You'd like to know whether we could offer you the purchase of one of your dreams from the future? A bit of tomorrow today? Some refreshment of that nature?"

"Yes. Precisely. Just as you have already done with Distelli, Lempytzka and others."

"I must disappoint you, dear Mr. Chief Inspector Stross. I cannot accommodate you. Your dreams can neither be caught nor sold."

"How can that be?"

"Simple. They're too wild, and I cannot catch them without great danger to myself. Instead of two fish there are four in your constellation. Two are on dry land. Besides, you are standing on two fish in motion. Bearing your feet upon them, they are swimming somewhere. All of this prevents me from hunting."

"And that's all you have to say to me?"

"No. I could recommend a horse for you to bet on next week..."

48

In my line of work I naturally have to take notes on the scene. Therefore I did so when I visited the "Symptom House" for the first time with Lempytzka. I recorded all that was said in the fake temple of Miss Klozewitz. I listened to a part of the tape yesterday and the words she said then sound unbelievable to me. I will quote a segment:

"Collective dreams existed and still do to this very day. Like when the long-legged feathered creatures of the swamp, such as snipes, bustards, herons and flamingos, multiply, making them easy to hunt, it is just as easy to hunt collective dreams when they multiply. They are everywhere. A good example are the dreams dreamt in choir by the Crusaders, eastern Romans and the Moslems in the 11th, 12th and 13th centuries, with the desire to conquer the Mediterranean. Those dreams of theirs were hunted in the timelessness and used relentlessly in the eighth, seventh and sixth centuries before Christ by dream merchants, and so they were collectively dreamt by the Phoenicians, Greek and Etruscans in their battle for rule over the western basin of the Mediterranean. Thus, those dreams about "naumahia" dreamed in the Mediterranean at the beginning of the second millennium after Christ were purchased and taken during the first millennium before Christ. They might, in the words of Jung, be called a "consequence of collective unconscious", only with one important difference. Collective unconscious in this case went from descendants to their distant ancestors, not the other way around, as Jung reasons when he deals with his cases of collective unconscious..."

49

I received a threatening letter today. It had a regular postal sign stamped upon it. It was sent from our town. It reads:

"Like a glass upon the table and a slice of drunken bread, so your tomorrow stands before you... You can stretch out your hand and take it, determine its color in the light, bite it and be intoxicated with it in advance. Like pillars of cold and hot scents in a sunny forest the hours of your tomorrow can already be seen today. And they can be counted like ribs. Just stretch out your hand and your finger is in his wound.

But you rather take nets and makeshifts, stretch out your tongue to see if it's raining, depart beneath the swift shade of a cloud, sit in your heart and instead of your own hunt another's tomorrow. As matters stand with you, better a sparrow in the bush than a bird in the hand."

All in all, that observing of tomorrow now reminds me of somebody. Of the "Symptom House" and Klozewitz. He offers the future today, and I seem to be threatened here for interfering in his business and hunting "another's tomorrow instead of my own".

50

One case from the Lempytzka-Distelli-Hecht-Erlangen proceedings has for now been proclaimed unsolved by the court. It is the matter of the murder at the hippodrome. I made up my mind on Friday and went straight to the big boss, "Sir Winston", as everybody calls him. He received me in his bookshop with a cigar behind his ear and silently gestured for me to take a seat with a hand that had no nails.

"Mr. Winston, you are reputed to know all about the secrets of this town. One might jest and say that you know in advance who will be killed here and when."

"They exaggerate!" said "Sir Winston" and wanted to laugh, but sneezed instead.

"That is certainly exaggerated, but I need your help to clarify a homicide that we have not been able to solve so far."

"What would you like to know, Mr. Stross?"

"Who killed Isaiah Cruise at the hippodrome?"

"What do you mean, who killed him? Distelli, of course. The opera singer."

"But Distelli was lying in hospital and dying of cancer at the time."

"Yak-yak-yak... dying of cancer he was, but he wasn't dead yet. He left the hospital for an hour to say farewell to his mistress, killed Cruise at the hippodrome and returned to his hospital bed to die. The perfect crime, is it not?"

"But where were his motives? Did he even know Cruise?"

"Ah, now that is a question for you, not myself... Would you like a cigar? I have "Partagas". They're excellent."

51

Some unknown person sent me a book by mail. It had blue covers and gilded letters indicating that is was from the "Do it Yourself" collection. The title was: How to Detect a Murderer? I was surprised to see that the book had only two pages of stiff paper and on them two pictures. One was a male bust with the hair, back of the head and collar drawn on, but no face. Instead of a parting there was a zipper in his hair, and instead of a face a tiny red *chain attached to the paper in the height of the parting at one end, and to the collar button at the other. It was long enough for its purpose, which I didn't detect straight away. On the other page there was a female bust with a bun, back of the head and pearl necklace drawn on, but also without a face, in place of which another chain was affixed. The book had a slit for a pen, but instead of a pen there was a pair of tweezers inside, explaining the whole thing: they were used to adjust the chain to "draw" and form a face. It was different every time.*

Somebody is leading me to the conclusion that the murderer I am to detect can be both male and female. Not either male or female, but precisely: both male and female.

52

In small towns by the sea there are lanes so narrow that two men could not pass one another. Such streets are called "let me through!" Well, there are such narrow passages within us as well, which get plugged up as soon as some other though of yours or somebody else's crowds into the slit as well. One such thread crept through my ears and I could almost hear it. Finally, after such a long time I solved my hardest and so far unsolved case of Distelli, Lempytzka, Hecht, Erlangen and Cruise!

Klozewitz was blackmailing Distelli, and then Lempytzka as well, selling them dreams from the future that prophesied to them a bit of what would happen to them before and after death. What did he ask of them in return? Only 1000 dollars each? Nonsense. He asked of them to commit murders. Of Distelli to kill Cruise, and of Lempytzka to murder her rival, namely the lover of Maurice Erlangen, Lady Hecht.

That is how it all happened, but nothing can be proven against Klozewitz, for neither Distelli nor Lempytzka are alive any more, the two of them that could have testified against him.

The only thing that remains incomprehensible is the question of the reasons and interest that Klozewitz had to remove Cruise and Lady Hecht in such a refined and complicated manner? Apart from witnesses to accuse him, this matter also lacks motive. Why them? And so Klozewitz can sleep peacefully on all three of my pillows.

53

I visited the apartment of the late Distelli on Thursday. There was nobody there in fact, but as soon as I rang the doorbell I heard the growling of Distelli's hound, and the neighboring door was opened to me by an old lady who said her name was Selina. I was astounded when she spoke.

"You can talk, dear Mrs. Selina! What a pleasant surprise," I said and stepped inside, "the late Lempytzka mentioned to me that you have been mute since birth!"

"She didn't have a clue. Would you like a drink, Mr. Chief Inspector? Walnut tea?... You haven't tried it? It's very tasty and unusual, you'll see."

While Selina was preparing the tea, I peeked under the lid of the grand piano that stood in the middle of the room. The piano was full of smoked pipes. I noticed a "Mogul", four Constantinople pipes of "sea foam", a dozen short sailor ones, some porcelain pipes with lids and two crafted specially to fit the hand that was to hold them. There were nargilehs there as well - one from Cairo, and the other from Tunis. I assumed that they were all Distelli's.

"What's your secret, Mrs. Selina?" I asked with a cup of walnut tea in my hand.

"You mean why was I silent for twenty years, so that everybody thought I was mute as a fish? Well, that's because of Distelli, or rather because of my grandmother Isidora. You see, she sang in the operetta in Vienna the century before last. A beautiful mezzo-soprano she had, and a lace parasol. Unfortunately she died of some severe inflammation of the throat. When Distelli became an *opera singer, I was terribly afraid that he, too, would perish from the throat. And in that fear I decided to sacrifice my own voice so that no harm would come to his throat. I stopped speaking... And it worked."*

"How do you mean it worked, Mrs. Selina? He died of cancer of the esophagus!"

"But no, Mr. Chief Inspector, by no means! He died of belly inflammation! Of a cancer metastasis on the stomach! When that happened, I began speaking immediately! It cannot be said that my sacrifice was in vain! By no means!"

"One more question, and then I will leave you to your care of Distelli's dog."

"Tamazar isn't a dog. He's a hound."

"And you, Mrs. Selina, what were you to the late Distelli?"

"How do you mean what was I to him? I was mother to him. But, Mr. Chief Inspector, I thought you would ask me something more important."

"What, Mrs. Selina?"

"About the murder at the hippodrome. You must have concerned yourself with that case as well. One afternoon while Distelli was lying in hospital, Marquezine Lempytzka came to my son's apartment, took his expensive "Combat Magnum" revolver and never again returned it. The betting-shop manager was killed the same evening. As far as I could tell from the papers, the murder was committed with the same kind of revolver - "Combat Magnum"..."

"Many thanks, dear Mrs. Selina. Is there anything else that you can recall concerning that case and Lempytzka?"

"One who has been silent for twenty years can be silent a while longer, Mr. Chief Inspector..."

As I was leaving my gaze happened to fall upon the bathroom. There was a huge tub inside, filled to the brim with dirty dishes and glasses.

54

One of the businessmen that I see around the hippodrome is Mr. Ishigumi, known by the nickname "the 50 dollar smile". I occurred to me to have a little chat with him. Here's how the conversation went:

"Mr. Ishigumi, were you at the hippodrome the evening that Isaiah Cruise was murdered?"

"I was."

"What were you doing there?"

"I live across the street from there and I'm always at home, except when I'm not."

"Did you see anything unusual that evening?"

"I did. I saw a woman in a red blouse and jeans enter the elevator and ascend to the 4th floor, meaning that she had the key to that floor, and such a key was only possessed, I suppose, by the betting-shop manager Isaiah Cruise."

"Does that mean that she killed him?"

"She didn't."

"How do you know?"

"When she climbed up there he was already dead. I had already heard three shots."

"Why did you not phone the police immediately?"

"I did. And your people at the police force learned of the death of Isaiah Cruise from me, and I didn't manage to see who killed him, for I was calling you just then."

And that 50 dollar smile of his spread across Mr. Ishigumi's face.

55

Among the witnesses in the Lempytzka case it never occurred to me to question Erlangen's assistant at the "Plusquam City" bank as well. I stopped by. The lady was a very beautiful Creole, one of those that would at the age of sixty still be not a day older than thirty. To my question about Lempytzka she replied in a voice of hot chocolate and she smelled of the perfume "Dune":

"Madam Lempytzka was one of the clients of our bank, of this high-security deposit box department in fact. I barely knew her, but of her I can tell you the following. The nutrition of a woman is strictly determined by her age. The nutrition is of one kind before the age of 15. From her 15th to her 25th year a woman needs quite a different sort of food. Between 25 and 35, if she continues with the feeding habits she was used to during the previous ten years, it will do her no good at all. In order to avoid disruptions she needs to change her form of nutrition entirely once more. I include here the beverages that she takes. The females of mammal species know all that instinctively and do not err. Lempytzka didn't know it, the food she took was quite the wrong kind and her organism and spirit suffered utter and lasting effects."

"How did that manifest itself in her case?"

"It's hard to keep track of everything, but I can tell you what it looked like in general. She mistook love for hunger, thirst for hatreds, thoughts for dreams, recollections for the future and jealousy for the fear of death..."

"Did she?" I blurted out just to say something, "and what were the consequences?"

"Unexpected. It did have some good sides, at least in a way."

"?"

"Women started to adore Lempytzka just as she was, as she became thanks to her erroneous nutrition. That within her attracted them irresistibly..."

At those words the Mulatto's sweat began smelling of hazelnuts.

As I left the "Plusquam City" bank I was completely confused. Was that conflict in the villa not perhaps a conflict of two women, Lady Hecht and Lempytzka, who were in love with one another, and not a conflict over their joint lover Erlangen?

56

Since I saw Alex Klozewitz for the first time in the courtroom (in the version with shaven head and a stud in his eyebrow), but never together with Miss Sandra whom I met at the "temple" of the "Symptom House", I decided to confront them. I told them that by telephone and announced my visit. He was sitting in the church, and she in the mirror across from him.

In greeting Miss Sandra Klozewitz said from the mirror:

"Alex and I are one being, we are not hermaphrodites, but androgyne, though you can only see that when you observe us in a mirror. Then our male nature separates from our female nature and divided into the figure in front of the glass and the one inside it... But that's not always the case and it isn't visible to everybody."

Sandra Klozewitz was perfectly made up, her eyebrows separated by an emerald stone, in her hair she wore a widespread fan sprinkled with stars, and she had gloves on her hands. But what gloves! At first I thought that the mirror reflected the light so as to make it seem like the girl in the looking-glass had seven fingers on one hand!

Then Miss Sandra laughed and said:

"You're marveling at my gloves? You're wondering whether my hand inside them has seven fingers as well? I shall not tell you that."

"Don't tell him anything!" exclaimed Klozewitz.

"No, I believe that the Chief Inspector has a right to know such things about fingers and the like..."

"You're playing games with your head, Sandra, both yours and mine. And stop doing that."

"But what's going on? I don't understand..." I interjected into this little argument. But it did no good. Alex concluded our conversation by rising to escort me to the door and Miss Klozewitz's reflection vanished from the mirror.

"Legally speaking, which one of you is the one fined for illegal gain of profit in the lawsuit with the sister of late Madam Lempytzka?" I asked Alex Klozewitz then.

"I'm afraid you'll have to decide for yourself which one of us is the real Klozewitz."

"Surely the one that knows the secret of the twelve fingers," I though on my way out.

57

Tonight, for the first time, I felt scared of my line of work which is known for the danger it brings. The Cruise-Lempytzka-Distelli-Klozewitz-Erlangen case scared me in particular. The matter seemed terribly threatening and it came to me in some kind of flash as I lay in bed, reading as usual to wind down and get myself to sleep after a strenuous day. In my hand I had the book that had been closest at hand, a book signed by some Z.L.N. and V.D.G., and it said something there that I read with horror and disbelief, as though it was literally referring to myself and the Lempytzka case that I was investigating, although it was actually referring to God-knows-what:

"The matter resembles shoving your hand into a bottomless bag, so that some strange thing is drawn from it every time, or something significant is at least touched or felt inside. And while there is some idea of how deep the hand can go, inserted as it is into the semi-darkness, the past seems real and tangible. Confusion arises when there is no more certainty of how far that "travel" has gone, and sometimes whether the hand has even remained at all..."

58

On Sunday, after one of those lunches with plenty of fats and spices, and whatever happens to be inside, I went for a stroll in Central Park. There I saw Mrs. Selina walking Distelli's regal hound. And then it came to me. A hound! Why yes, a hound!

Where was it that I came across another hound? Of course, in the dream! What does that dream mean for my investigation? Who is the hound to Distelli? His double with their joint mistress Lempytzka! In Lempytzka's dream a white hound appears under a wild cherry tree. The hound beneath that tree is sleeping in the cupboard. He is a lover unawoken as yet there. So the hound is Distelli's double.

And what else? Who is the hound with the golden head from the dream on Pushkin to Distelli? As opposed to the regal white hound which is Distelli's double in love, who is the one on Pushkin's divan, stretched out as if on a psychiatrist's couch - the one with the golden head? Distelli walks on tiptoe around him in the dream in fear of waking him, for even in the dream he knows that the hound, as soon as it wakes, will slay somebody...

That isn't so difficult to figure out either. Distelli was a handsome man with a golden mane that glistened in the sunlight like a halo. Therefore that hound with the golden hound is Distelli as well. But the hound with the golden head is not a lover. Distelli was, in fact, afraid of awakening a murderer inside him who would slay somebody. Whom?

Both Distelli and Lempytzka are afraid of becoming murderers, therefore they knew in advance what they were going to do and why. And I still don't know.

59

So far I have found no connections nor motives that would link the Distelli-Lempytzka case with the murder *of Isaiah Cruise at the hippodrome. Who could have come into possession of Distelli's "Magnum" with which the murder was committed while he was lying in hospital on his deathbed? A neighbor more than fifty years old, who feeds his dog, and Lempytzka, his mistress, who would sometimes come to kiss the dog and then leave. They both had a key to Distelli's apartment. Perhaps the idea of the neighbor should not be rejected entirely, though she seems quite harmless at first glance.*

So I seeked her out.

As we were drinking tea, I started chatting:

"Dear Mrs. Selina, I searched and did not find an explanation for an unclear part of Madam Lempytzka's dream. Klozewitz's report says the following about that part: "warm blood surged through him bearing with it like a shadow some other network, not of blood circulation but something much, much older, the flow of something ancient that has been running through human bodies for millions of years..." I've been struggling for a long time over what that "something else", that "shadow of blood circulation" that is much older than any living creature might be? What do you think?"

"Piece of cake. That, dear Mr. Chief Inspector, is time! It has been running through our arteries and veins since forever, for every child is born with inherited dreams of others within him... But let's leave off the trivia. I shall reveal to you something more important about that report that Klozewitz put together for the court and yourself. The dream that Klozewitz submitted to the court as one supposedly dreamt by Lempytzka is nothing but a forgery!"

60

In timeless space (where dreamed and undreamt dreams float) the future and the past are interwoven, for there is no present to separate them, just as is the case in dreams. There is no present in dreams either, but the tomorrow and the yesterday are joined.

With such thoughts I observed the design of the sky. Upon gazing at the gathering of celestial bodies in the constellation of my sign, "Pisces", I was horrified to realize that up there in the Universe of my zodiac there was no present.

I made inquiries about my sign of the zodiac. In Indian maps of the sky there really are four instead of two fish, as was brought to my attention by Klozewitz. I found out something else as well. In astrological manuscripts those fish are sometimes portrayed as having letters instead of scales. Such is the case with the sign of "Pisces" in a manuscript from the 10th century in which the fish are covered not by scales but by letters, and so spell out a Greek myth in the Latin language. There is also the belief that each fish has different letters on its scales as well as that there were astrologers in the past who could still remember how those letters could be read. I believe that they still exist today. But today there is nobody that can explain the purpose of man.

In conclusion I might add that Klozewitz, as an astrologer, can decipher me whenever he wants, but I cannot decipher him. At least for now. Not at all flattering for a chief inspector. However I might consider Klozewitz to be a charlatan, a crook and a fraud, he has obviously infected me.

61

There is something unclear about Distelli's golden snuff-egg. Was it stolen as Lempytzka told me? Who stole it and when? Was it at the time of the breaking and entering into Distelli's apartment? What was in it? Where is it now?

With those questions I went to the "mute" Mrs. Selina, of whom it is said that she did not speak for 20 years. The answer was incredible:

"Dear Mr. Chief Inspector, do you know what an egg is?

The yolk is sleep, and the white is wake. Sleep feeds upon our wake, and when it is strong enough, it breaks the shell and flies away. It's the same with Distelli's golden egg as well..."

62

Erlangen defended himself in court by claiming of some witness, whose name was Erwin and who was present at Lempytzka's murder. That witness had been prepared to testify that Erlangen had fired in self-defense, but he failed to appear in court and could not be located at the number he gave Erlangen. I thought (as did the judges) that Erlangen had made this witness up. Now, however, I'm beginning to think that this might not be so. At the murder of Isaiah Cruise at the hippodrome there was also a witness, a woman in a red blouse and jeans who happened to be on the spot immediately after Cruise's murder. This is vouched for by Mr. Ishigumi, called "the

50 dollar smile", who lives nearby and who reported the murder to the police. Can it be considered a coincidence that both murders were practically committed in front of witnesses? Was somebody monitoring the murderers? Somebody obviously wanted to verify that they had completed their tasks.

63

I went to Lempytzka's apartment again. This time without a search warrant. I didn't need one. I was let in and left in the semi-darkness that smelled of moldy pianos, of last year and tomorrow's rain. I sat and listened to the device mincing winds in the window. In the drawer of a table with hoofs instead of legs I found a notebook. It was strangely twisted into a tube encompassed by a dog collar. Inside, on a receipt from an aromatic herb shop, there was a poem written in Lempytzka's handwriting:

*Your face I have long since loved and known,
All my life I have followed the trail left behind
By your paws and the brush of your tail in the snow.
You're a bird transformed into beast, I know
Only in death shall your feathers be shown
And paw-prints into a bird's trail turn
Along which I can once more return.*

Can you believe it! Did Lempytzka write a love poem to the hound of her lover Distelli?

64

The night before last it occurred to me that I never once asked myself during the investigation into the Lempytzka-Klozewitz case what the financial standing of the two of them was. Namely, was Lempytzka in debt and what was the situation at the "Symptom House" in this respect - did it have debts or not? Does it pay to sell dreams and trade in the future? It's a bit unusual and quite expensive to build a church instead of a conference room for board meetings, or whatever it is that they hold there. Was it paid for in cash? Or in installments? And who were they indebted to, if indeed they were?

Naturally, I went to late Lady Hecht's "Plusquam City" bank first. With a warrant. They were not too pleased to assist me, but when they hear that the police was only looking for a "yes" or "no" answer to the question of whether the "Symptom House" had taken loans from them, they rushed to check in their computers. The reply was - no! They had never done business with such a company, and so could have incurred no debts with their bank.

Then, seemingly in passing, I asked the question that was the real reason for my visit - whether Lempytzka had debts in that bank, for I thought that a connection might be made in that manner with the murder of their chairwoman Lady Hecht. To the question of whether the late Madam Lempytzka had been a client and whether she owed any sum of money to the bank, they replied that they had never had any business connections with her, apart from the high-security deposit box department, where she rented a safe...

And all the while they looked at me with the same horror in their eyes as in those of a turtle looking on from its shell at a bird of prey that carries it up to the heights and drops it to smash on a rock in order to eat it more easily.

65

This matter occurred during my first visit to the "Symptom House" when Lempytzka and I were received by Miss Sandra. While she was occupied with asking Lempytzka whether she had any family ties with Lempytzka the painter, I noticed as I sat in the pew of the church that it had drawers of the kind used to store prayer books. I covertly eased the drawer open and peeked inside. It was half-empty. Which means that I did see something inside after all. It surprised me, for instead of a prayer book or some such object I saw a transparent cigar tube bearing only half of the label: "...tagas". And now I ask myself who smokes "Partagas" there, for Klozewitz does not smoke at all, and how come that object happened to be there, unless a client of the "Symptom House" left it behind, etc. I only know that "Partagas" in such transparent packaging is smoked by "Sir Winston" and that this could perhaps mean (if the "Partagas" cigar tube originated from him) that there was some connection between Klozewitz and "Sir Winston".

Being transparent, it was plain to see that there were at least three "ifs" next to one another in that tube... And this brings further investigation in that direction up against a wall of silence.

66

The flowers in the silver teapot suspended from the ceiling are gently swaying. Tonight, as I look at that teapot, I believe that silence is always full of words. What was kept silent in the Lempytzka case? What could have been kept silent? How did Klozewitz record those dreams? Did he really, as he claims, acquire and sell them, or did Distelli and Lempytzka simply recant those dreams to him from a couch like they would any psychiatrist? And then Klozewitz recorded his version of those dreams on tape? Did he first censor Lempytzka's dream on footsteps in the version that he submitted to us? Did Klozewitz erase from the tape some parts that might discredit him in any way? That would be very difficult to determine. And he knows it.

67

The rain is coming to an end outside, I feel tired, the moon is appearing, cut in half, and sleep will not come over my eyes. Some kind of halftime flows and I crawl into bed, having first grabbed the closest book I could reach, determined to read for a while in bed. It's a German book of some kind, I don't know when I bought it, nor why, but inside it I find a large inky signature across an entire page, the author's inscription to me. Then I recall that it's a book bought in an attempt to find out from the author something of use in a case that I was unable to solve, that this is "my page" of the book and that it would be interesting to see at least a few words of what is written inside, for the author mentioned that the lines might bear a personal message for me. Perhaps they have some message about the Lempytzka-Hecht-Klozewitz-Distelli case as well, which I might be interested in... I also recall the brief conversation between the author and myself on that occasion:

"Could you give me a piece of advice? What is a man to do if he keeps running up against a wall whichever way he turns?

"What kind of wall? A wall of lament?"

"No, I run into a wall of silence everywhere. What should I do?"

"You shall have to be silent a bit as well," he retorted...

Remembering those words, I open the book and die before I begin to read. In the morning I awake and realize that the dreamed death was not real, although it is still a bit of practice for dying. In any case the path before me has become shorter than the one left behind, and I don't know when that came to pass.

68

An expert in Russian romanticism, whose advice I sought on the matter of Matheas Distelli's dream about Pushkin's death, submitted to me (on the basis of Alexander Klozewitz's report on the dreams) a notification that he found two more traces of poems that really are Pushkin's in the dream. The linguist that came before him (whom I also asked for his professional opinion) did not notice them. The following words from the dream: "Be quiet! You are young and stupid, you will not hunt me down!" are actually a quote from Pushkin's work "Scenes from Faust", and the short poem "Peasants here are rich aplenty..." is actually a chant from "Eugene Onegin".

I paid him and spat. That would be of no use for my investigation. But the question arises of who was so familiar with Pushkin's opus? Distelli's subconscious or Klozewitz? Or yet a third person?

69

I do not settle for defeat, but victory no longer brings me joy. I counted my fears tonight. There are more of them than there are the Lord's commandments. It is well known that the most dangerous man in town is "Sir Winston", but I am somehow more afraid of Klozewitz.

The Lempytzka case constantly invokes in my insomnia the recollection of a beautiful woman putting something cold and heavy in my hand and saying, indicating that it would be better for me:

"I give you a lie so that you neither say black nor white, neither it is nor it isn't, neither day nor night, neither I will not I won't, neither yes nor no, neither you are nor you aren't..."

And in my semi-slumber I realize that being a chief inspector is incompatible with such advice.

70

As I read in the evening before going to bed I came across a story entitled "Two Fans from Gallata". I didn't even look at it. I threw the book down and grabbed hold of the list *of objects that the computer had comprised for me to use in the investigation of the Lempytzka case. As "corpus delicti" the list also contained the fan of Miss Sandra Klozewitz, decorated with stars from the constellation "Cancer". What is the meaning of this group of stars above her head? A Cancer, as is well known, loves his home and sticks to it. He will do anything to preserve and improve it. Is that a sign that the Klozewitz couple (if they might be called that) is prepared to do anything and will stop at nothing to preserve their home, the "Symptom House"? In which manner and from which direction could they be jeopardized so that their property, namely their house, would come into question? Debts? There is no answer, but if such a threat did exist, Klozewitz was surely not in doubt for a moment as to what he would sacrifice - his home or somebody's life. Unfortunately, that is all I can squeeze out from Miss Sandra's fan. It is folded, though the stars on it are visible.*

71

When Maurice Erlangen was released on parole, I gave orders for him to be tailed just in case. I wanted to know where he would go first after serving his sentence. They informed me as soon as he departed somewhere by car from his villa. I followed him: he drove straight to the "Midnight Sun" inn. And there was a woman waiting for him there. I had never before seen a kiss like the one she greeted him with. It was Sandra Klozewitz. When I glanced into the mirror that should have reflected the male side of her androgyne nature, to my surprise Alex Klozewitz could not be seen in the glass. He was not present in

Sandra's life that day and there was nobody in the looking glass with shaven head and a stud in his eyebrow kissing with Erlangen. Both in front of the mirror and inside it Erlangen was kissing a gorgeous woman with a fan in her hair, sprinkled with stars from the constellation "Cancer". And one more thing. As far as I could tell, she was wearing her heady scent "Antracite" that day...

Faced with that scent and the kiss I felt terrible. Completely useless and superfluous in the world. And I realized who I was. I was the one into whose palm other spit when he works and into whose plate when he eats. From one of my pockets grows wheat, from the other grass, rains falls into my bowl, and snow into my bed. I was the one that combs with a fork, the one that plants knives and fattens teeth, for spoons do not sprout when I eat. They gave me wine in a bell - If I drink it does not ring, if it rings I do not drink...

72

The night before last I had an unexpected and unbelievable visit. The sister of late Madam Lempytzka, Miss Sophia Androsovich showed up in my apartment.

"Did anybody tell you that your door handles tear sleeves and that your left eye is slower than your right? That, dear Mr. Chief Inspector, means," added my guest, sprawling into the nearest armchair, "that you can see two things at the same time which is your advantage, but at the same time an entire unsolved police case can slip in between your two views of the world..."

"You flatter me, Miss Androsovich."

"Yes, that's true. But that isn't why I came. I am here because I forgot to mention in court that this actually did happen to you. In between your two views of the world you missed something essential for the Lempytzka & Co. case.

"?"

"You don't know what? In this entire game that we are all playing - both the living and the dead, from my sister Lempytzka & Co. to yourself, Chief Inspector, there is somebody who is neither seen nor mentioned, yet holds all the threads in his hands. Somebody who planned this entire mix-up. Do you know who that is?"

"?"

"I will tell you. It is somebody who knows what you secretly write in your blue book and can read every line inside it whenever he wants. He might be doing so this very minute! I know that you have put me, too, into that booklet of yours, but that one could stuff me and you together with your book into his pocket and forget us there forever."

And with disgust Miss Androsovich picked up, using two fingers, the blue book into which I am writing these words now and waved it in front of my face. Then she took out a bottle from her handbag and sprinkled scent over all three of my pillows with the words:

"Come, love, I'll tear this bachelor bed of yours apart."

73

I passed by a store window tonight and saw a book inside that had the following inscription:

NEW!!! THE NOVEL "UNIQUE ITEM"

The author of "Dictionary of the Khazars" has once more found a new, as yet unseen type of literary play for you: a delta novel!

It's a tale of love and a detective "multi-ending story" that diverges into one hundred branches and leads you towards one hundred different endings. Every reader obtains his personal one.

You have a UNIQUE ITEM!

To my amazement, there was a picture of a "Combat Magnum" revolver on the cover of the book. And of precisely the same rare and expensive type that Isaiah Cruise, Lady Hecht and Lempytzka were killed with - a Distinguished Combat Magnum, model 586, in metallic blue steel, with a handle of carved wood!

Did somebody already write a novel about the case of Madam Lempytzka and her lover Maurice Erlangen before I had time to solve it? What speed! Time ages fast in our century. You rise on Monday, and retire on Saturday, you can wake up famous and go to bed forgotten, and somebody stole your yesterday before you had time to blink.

74

I dreamed of Lempytzka. She was sitting by a computer at the huge St. Petersburg airport that was completely vacant. Dawn had only just broken outside. I don't know if she was waiting for a plane, or was part of the staff there. She didn't even notice me, as though she were alone. In her left hand she was clutching an American anti-stress ball, and with her right she was embroidering beautiful tablecloths, curtains and pillow samples in the computer design program. As soon as one was completed, she would erase it by hitting the "delete" button and start a new one immediately. The same pattern could be seen on all the "embroideries" - stars from the constellation "Cancer".

Was Lempytzka trying to draw my attention to Alex(S)andra Klozewitz in this manner as well, and let me know that (s)he was to blame for everything, as she had claimed while she had been alive?

75

I have long since given my computer the task to list all of the objects mentioned during the inquest and in court at the Lempytzka & Co. proceedings. Every "corpus delicti" or anything that might be termed as such was entered. I looked them over the night before last and singled out the following four:

- Miss Sandra Klozewitz's fan,
- Distelli's golden snuff-egg,
- The purple scarf from Lempytzka's safety deposit box, and
- The transparent tube labeled "Partagas" glimpsed for an instant in a drawer at the "Symptom House" "temple".

I estimated that it would be best for me to look into the matter of Distelli's golden snuff-egg first. It was the egg that supposedly (according to Lempytzka's oral statement) disappeared from Distelli's apartment at the time of the breaking and entering. But let's leave the B & E for *now. Distelli was a sniffer, then. What did he sniff? Was it merely snuff, or something more than that? Cocaine?*

I immediately arranged for a meeting with "Felix" - our man at the opera who was in charge of monitoring the supply of narcotics that entered this sphere.

"Did Distelli buy anything from you?"
"Yes."
"Cocaine?"
Felix giggled.
"Oh no, he bought pot, and rarely. It seems that he was resistant to drugs. They didn't grab him. It was more of a "pose". So it could be said that Distelli, too, "smoked"."
"He was a harmless case, then?"
"Light offences here and there. Of no significance to our program."
"Are you sure that he didn't have some other dealer apart from yourself, a real one? Whom you were inadvertently "covering for"?"
"I don't think so. I wouldn't have missed it... Wait a minute... What did he keep his snuff in? A purse, or a metal box?"
"A metal egg."
"A silver snuff-box?"
"No. It was made of gold."
"Blimey! I can't believe it!"
"Why?"
"Cocaine reacts with silver and spoils. That's why it's kept in a golden container, with which no chemical compound can be formed."
"So it's possible that he fooled you and led us all by the nose, buying pot from you occasionally, yet actually buying "heavier stuff", namely cocaine, from some other, real, dealer...

You, dear Felix, have a man to catch in the vicinity of the opera. I, unfortunately, do not. Mine is deceased."

76

As is already written somewhere in this diary, I went to the "Plusquam City" bank the other day and checked out the safety deposit box of the late Lempytzka. Inside it I found a purple scarf... Why would somebody lease a specially secured deposit box in the most reputed bank in town in order to place a single scarf inside? That scarf will lie there in the box for as long as Miss Sophia Androsovich, the sister of the late Lempytzka, pays for it, if indeed she does. Then the safe will be opened in front of witnesses, its contents will be officially determined and handed over to her inheritors, if the court finds that there are any and that the purple scarf belongs to them... That scarf still needs to be thought about once more and placed on the list of objects that might be corpus delicti.

77

It occurred to me that God shall be witness of whether Erlangen should have served time, for he might not have overstepped necessary self-defense when he shot Lempytzka. Perhaps Lempytzka really had been intending to kill Erlangen as well and perhaps she had even aimed and fired a blank, for who knows if she even counted the bullets directed at Lady Hecht. In that case she had not been aware at the time of firing at Erlangen that there were no more bullets in her "Magnum", that it was empty. He could not have known that either.

That would mean that Erlangen's claim that he and Lempytzka fired simultaneously was the truth. And that he was the victim of yet another court error... But in that case we have at least two "ifs".

78

I decided to telephone Miss Sandra Klozewitz. I picked up the receiver and said:

"Last time you mentioned, Miss Sandra, some secret about fingers. Let me remind you, you were wearing a glove with seven fingers on your left hand, therefore there was a total of twelve fingers on your hands. You must admit that this is most unusual. The matter has been intriguing me and so I would like to ask you for a brief explanation."

"I shall tell you something about it, although Alex feels that it might jeopardize us. I, however, believe that if I were to reveal that secret about fingers to somebody, it might even protect us..."

"It might, but posthumously!" sniggered Alex and so I realized that he was following our conversation as well.

"Believe me, Miss Sandra," I interjected, "the police will take all precautions to protect you in case you find yourself in danger. But tell me, what kind of danger might this be?"

"Oh, you didn't quite understand me. It's not a matter of danger that is threatening us personally. I'm talking about our profession, about astrologers in general. During your previous visit you saw those gloves on me. Those were astrological gloves. One is always seven-fingered, and the other has five fingers, making, together with the first one with seven, a total of a dozen fingers, meaning that I have a finger for each month of the year. For each sign of the zodiac as well, therefore. And so my fingers are, by means of the astrological gloves, connected to the Universe and celestial bodies... And now we are getting to the point. If somebody decides to inflict an injury upon some astrologer, or us, he would most probably start from the fingers. They are the most sensitive parts to us. If one of our fingers were to be cut off, we wouldn't be crippled like you would if somebody cut your finger off. We would become double cripples. Apart from remaining with a defective hand, we would lose the power to establish astrological contact with the Universe and our dream hunting grounds for an entire zone, for that zone covered by the zodiacal sign that we had been connected with by the finger that, after the mutilation, we no longer have... That is the story of the gloves," concluded Miss Sandra and added:

"If you ever hear that somebody somewhere has cut of someone's, say, little finger - think, dear Mr. Chief Inspector, what that might mean altogether and search for the culprit at triple speed. For, he will not stop at the fingers..."

As I left this chat line, the same question kept occurring to me: who was it that would want to harm Klozewitz and why? And I had no answer. Yet both of them knew it very well. And kept their mouths shut all the same.

79

I took another look at the list of "objects" that the computer comprised as possible "evidence" in the Klozewitz and Lempytzka case. I noticed that the list didn't contain the stud that Klozewitz wore in his eyebrow. Yet precisely this stud had been mentioned the day that Lempytzka and I met and went to visit the "Symptom House".

After the visit Lempytzka and I exchanged a few words on the street in parting. I asked her:

"Did you notice a man in the "church" while we were talking to Miss Sandra Klozewitz?"

"I didn't. I had the feeling that we were alone."

"Oh... Strange, very strange, Madam Lempytzka. And did you notice that Miss Sandra keeps a mirror in her "temple"?"

"Yes."

"And did you notice anything unusual in the mirror?"

"No. Apart from the fact that it was hanging in a church, but it's a "so-called church" anyway."

"You know, the mirror was turned in such a direction that only Miss Sandra Klozewitz could be seen in it."

"Well?"

"You see, that's the point. Instead of Miss Sandra's reflection in the mirror I saw the reflection of a man with a shaven head and a stud in his eyebrow. Did you notice that as well?"

"No. And I was staring at the mirror, because Miss Sandra gazed at herself in it every once in a while, adjusting that ridiculous fan of hers. You must have been seeing things..."

Now I believe that Lempytzka saw in the mirror what she expected to be seen in it, while I noticed what *really had been there in the looking glass, namely a man with a stud in his eyebrow.*

At this moment the late Lempytzka would surely also be able to see that man in the mirror, whose name is Alex Klozewitz and who is, in some unproven way, guilty of her death.

80

During *the hearing after the murder at the villa I asked Erlangen:*

"What was your relationship with Lempytzka?"

"Most cordial."

"What does that mean?"

"I was screwing her."

"And Lady Hecht?"

"Her I humped."

"What's the difference?"

"You ought to know what that means. You're a grown man. Lady Hecht I banged as though she were a man, and Lempytzka as a woman."

"Why did you kill Lempytzka?"

"In self-defense. We fired at the same time."

"There were no bullets in her revolver. Why should she shoot? It was empty."

"I could not have known that."

"So you say... But I wanted to ask you one last thing. Did you ask Lempytzka to kill Lady Hecht?"

"Of course not. She killed her out of jealousy. But a chief inspector shouldn't ask questions for which he knows in advance that an affirmative reply cannot be the truth."

81

I met a friend of the late Lempytzka. I asked her what they had talked about the last time they had seen each other.

"I don't remember exactly. She was rather weird."
"?"
"She used weekends as some kind of "viagra", and Mondays as penicillin... The last time we met I believe I asked her something like: why does an orgasm last longer for some people and shorter for others.

"Because," she replied, "the present lasts longer for some, and shorter for others, for some death is longer, and for others shorter.""

"For a smart man two words are enough, and three too little!" I thought as I took my leave.

82

I enquired at the prison whether Erlangen had received mail, and from whom. Of all that they placed at my disposal I found his amorous letters the most interesting. Only one woman wrote to him and I concluded from her postcard that they had never met before. The woman signed the card with the initials "R. Alfa" and she had begun writing to him after she had seen Erlangen's picture in the newspapers and read all about his case. She felt that he had been convicted innocent and she wished to make the sentence easier for him to bear with her letters. What he wrote to her was naturally unknown, but judging from one of her letters that had been opened, for it had contained a solid object, and was thus seen by the prison authorities, she sent him love verses and expected them to meet as soon as he was let out of jail. Here are the verses from the letter:

> When all it has given time retrieves
> Truth shall then come to take for itself,
> But what it has given too scant it believes,
> It will take back more than it gives.
>
> From all things the secret is slowly revealed,
> And I see them nude as myself they displayed
> On you the veil still gleams unconcealed
> You are secluded by unsoiling shade
> And only inside you my secret still lives.

83

I realized later on that Klozewitz has a perfectly developed sense of smell. People even talk about it. On one occasion Lempytzka told me the following as if she were revealing to me some "corpus delicti" against Klozewitz:

"That one can smell the stench of chickens from Kish's book "Early Woes" and buffalo dung from Pablo Picasso's drawing."

I remember those words well, but I don't of whom else I recently read (or dreamt?) that he has just as fine a nose... Who was it? In the morning I will instruct the computer to rake through Distelli's and Lempytzka's dreams until it finds out who there, in the dreams, has a fine sense of smell...

84

From the love letters that Erlangen was exchanging from prison with an unknown person, I found out only her signature, which was some kind of code - "R. Alfa". I informed myself in computer encyclopedia about everything connected with the letter Alfa. And so I came to the conclusion that R. Alfa could most probably be an abbreviation from the field of astrology, and resolved it spells out: "rektascenzia Alfa", which would comply with the zodiacal sign of "Cancer". Thus the woman who wrote Erlangen love letters while he was in prison was born under the sign of "Cancer", and so the back of her letters, instead of a name and address, contained the five stars that make up the fork-like celestial constellation of "Cancer".

*

*
*

*

*

I asked myself straight away where I had seen that sign recently? Stars aligned just so? Of course, I remembered the "Cancer" on the fan of Miss Sandra Klozewitz...

85

Androgyne Alex Klozewitz, when he appears in his male nature, has a shaven head. Who else in this story of Lempytzka & Co. has a shaven head? And what does it mean?

That, of course, is not hard to detect. In Distelli's dream on Pushkin, the Pretender Grishka Otrepyev shaves his head to avoid the spells that Pushkin cast upon him with his African needles. However, Distelli's dream on Pushkin, even though it's at our disposal in full, doesn't say whether the Pretender Grishka Otrepyev was a devil or not?

Therefore, the only reliable fact that we have is that Klozewitz wore a shaven head to avoid somebody casting a spell, evil eye, witchcraft of a curse upon him. Who and why?

86

The assistant investigator that arrested Erlangen on the spot, responding to his telephone call from the villa, concluded at first that Erlangen had committed both of the murders, that of Lady Hecht and of Marquezine Lempytzka.

In his opinion the event took place in the following manner: Erlangen arrived with two "Magnums" and in gloves. He committed the murder of Lady Hecht with one "Magnum", and used the other to kill Lempytzka, and then put the "Magnum" with which he killed Lady Hecht into Lempytzka's hands. Thus her fingerprints were found on that weapon, and he himself confessed that he had shot at Lempytzka in self-defense.

The assumption is interesting, but it fell flat after the ballistics and other investigations that were undertaken later on.

87

The court documents concerning the case of Lempytzka, Klozewitz & Co. contain the information of when Klozewitz was born. He was born in the month of April and his zodiac sign is "Aries". If one was to seek out the sign that was the most intolerant towards "Aries", one would find that it was "Cancer". And that is the very sign that Sandra Klozewitz bears upon her fan.

Is it possible that androgyne beings have different signs of the zodiac depending on whether they are turned towards the male of the female side, the Sun or the Moon?

88

The ricochet from Distelli's dream about Pushkin is occupying my mind once more. It is the basic thread of the dream - so you could say. What is the message of that dream in fact? Who in the Distelli-Lempytzka case is aimed at, even hit, but the bullet rebounds off some polished object on the chest of the unknown person and turns, leaving the one it was intended for unharmed? Ricochet! In my investigation somebody was missed, but should have been hit. Who? Was it somebody unknown who is now in possession of Distelli's golden egg?

89

I met Miss Sophia Androsovich again yesterday, the sister of the late Lempytzka. She looked at me with her beautiful speckled eyes and said as we were sitting over an upper:

"Did you notice that the day you were born isn't the same in your sleep as when you're awake? In our sleep our date of birth moves thousands of years into the past. Our immortality, therefore, begins before our birth and can infinitely be measured backwards through time. It's perhaps the only immortality that we shall have. Thus in our sleep we are not only older than during our waking hours, we are immortal. I don't know if time lives in the future, but I know for certain that it exists no more in the past. Maybe that which we call the future is actually just an illness of time. And in the past there is only eternity. With you at the bottom..."

"And how do you explain the Klozewitz case? Alex and Sandra have different birth dates not only in their sleep, but during their waking hours as well. His is in the sign of "Aries" and hers in the sign of "Cancer". Can an androgyne being have two dates of birth? One for the male, and the other for the female side of its nature?"

"I rather wouldn't talk about Klozewitz. I'll only tell you that their birth dates are differently calculated than ours. That's all."

90

I've been grabbed by the mania of invoking spirits once more. Since I received ten or so days of leave, I took a ticket to Cairo determined to seek out in the Copt part of the city the fortuneteller Zoida recommended to me in Paris. I found her under some eaves near the Copt church, painting women's eyes in the Egyptian fashion.

"You would like me to invoke somebody's shade from the dead?" she asked me as soon as we found ourselves alone.

"Yes."

"What is the person's name?"

"Marquezine Androsovich Lempytzka."

"What sign was she born under?"

"The sign of "Aquarius"."

"Did you know her personally?"

"Yes."

"What is the question that you would like to ask her?"

"Who is to blame for her death."

"Do you have any object that she possessed, or a book that she read?"

I had been warned of such a request by those that had sent me to the fortuneteller in Cairo, and so I took from my pocket and handed her a letter from Marquezine's father to Marquezine. Zoida placed her hand on the letter, closed her eyes and told me:

"In order for you to invoke her it is important for you to "purify" yourself and open up to her, not expecting her to be open to you."

"How do you do that?"

"Whenever you dream somebody else's dream, that morning you are "pure"."

"How can I tell if I've dreamt somebody else's dream?"

"It happens to everybody and isn't all that rare. Only people pay no attention to it and forget everything immediately. If you dream other people's dreams you can tell by the fact that somebody else wakes up *in them before you do. And those that awaken in the dreams of others choose dreams that don't smell and are not dirty for that purpose. If they choose yours, it means that you're "pure" that day, and Lempytzka will be able to recognize you and come to you. After you wake up try to remember as precisely as possible what Lempytzka looked like. From then on commences her reply to your question."*

"In what form will I receive it?"

"You'll spell it out with your own hand. First you need to write down your "energies" such as: love, sadness, cold and such and mark them with letters of the alphabet as each one occurs to you. After that it's all simple. Every day you will write down which "energy" came to you first. Whether you were cold that morning, or had a toothache, or felt hunger, thirst, heat etc. Since you've already marked all those "energies" with letters of the alphabet, it won't be hard to read what Madam Lempytzka has to say..."

After that I went to the pyramids in Giza almost certain that it would never again occur to me to delve in invoking spirits. Zoida took my hands in hers in parting and gazed into my eyes:

"Take care! If you manage to invoke her, it will not end well for you."

91

Last week I received a call from the lawyer that had represented Sophia Androsovich, Lempytzka's sister, in the lawsuit against Klozewitz. He had something to tell me regarding that case.

"You see. Mr. Chief Inspector, during her lifetime I represented Madam Lempytzka as well. At one point she wanted to sue Klozewitz for sexual relations against her will and for fraud. She informed me of that before one of her trips."

"Where did she travel to? Cairo?"

"Yes. With her lover at the time, Erlangen."

"So why didn't you file charges?"

"When she returned she decided not to sue Klozewitz after all. She said that she had made it all up."

92

Only later did I remember to ask Miss Sophia Androsovich (sister of the late Lempytzka) whether she possessed anything that had belonged to her sister. She told me that I was prodding in an unhealed wound, mentioned that they had grown up never knowing their father, whom their mother had kept far from the two of them. Only after his death had they been informed that their father had known their names, that he had written to them, but not knowing where to send those lines had left them in his small archive which had been inherited by Sophia Androsovich. She gave me a letter that their father had written to Lempytzka:

> Dear unknown daughter,
> My beloved Marquezine,
> One night in France your mother showed me how well she could dance the tango, but she admitted to me that she wasn't interested in the words that accompanied it. She

said then that love poetry, from its very origin, has not been addressed to women at all (apart from a few verses written by Sapfo and some other female poets), but is pure male rivalry and strutting which is meant to show who of the males has a finer peacock tail and a better cornucopia. And so, she said then, poetry did not interest her, for it didn't apply to her. Besides, she concluded, one dances to music and not to words...

I have found something that might be called a "Lesson in Poetry Reading" and I send you those verses more to remind you of the said conversation between your father and your mother, than to teach you how to read poetry. This is the only reason that I send you this poem. I did not write it, but am merely copying it out for you:

> Come, I shall teach you how a poem is read.
> Enter. There, now join, and stretch out your hands.
> Well? Are you swallowing? Your chin
> Up and forward. Not overly upstream,
> Be careful towards that flow:
> That water might easily drown inside you.
> Words aim at their shadows
> And when they hit they vanish, or say:
> "Come anywhere, but be on time!"
> Hard, isn't it? We're closest when we aren't still.
> Now place a hair between your calves.
> Perhaps you will find two tomorrow
> As if you planted something that gave fruit
> In the meanwhile. If you return.
> For you wake in the morning, and don't even dream yet
> Who's already had the chance to slap you.

93

I noticed long ago that during the investigation I didn't (apart from the official report on Distelli's death) dive deeper into the matter of his status at the hospital and during the hospital treatment. Why didn't I-I wonder - talk to his doctors about his behavior at the time? For example, was he receiving psychiatric attention at the hospital? Private fellow professor Dr. Arnold Getz, whom I visited there yesterday, kindly gave me a reply to those questions. He, as a psychiatrist, attended to Distelli.

"Of course he told me about his dream related to Pushkin," he remarked immediately, "I noticed in that dream that great attention was paid to Pushkin's family tree and the poet's ancestors. Even the African needles that are a lever to pressure others and obtain what you want by force are inherited in the dream from the Russian poet's great-grandfather. In order to understand those elements of Distelli's dream, let's recall that in psychiatry things can be observed within the individual unconscious (Freud), collective unconscious (Jung) and the family unconscious (Szombi). We shall not dwell now on how the third and youngest method of the family unconscious was received in science. It seems here that we have a case that says that Distelli had, or felt that he had somebody in the family from whom he had inherited the power to force others around him ("demons" in his dream) to do what he was interested in. From that point of view it would be very significant to research whether it was all just a dream, or if there was true historical fact in that part of the dream on Pushkin concerning the poet's great-grandfather.

If the dream about Pushkin's ancestor was a figment of Distelli's subconscious, that would indicate that Distelli inherited some family inclination towards violence in order to force the persons in his surroundings to meet his desires and intentions. However, if that sequence of Distelli's dream was based on historical facts that might have reached him through literature and history, it would have quite a different meaning and lead to other conclusions. But in order to resolve that we shall need a historian..."

And so Dr. Arnold Getz concluded our conversation and I packed up, uncertain of whether to continue drilling a hole from which one would want out.

94

During the proceedings the sister of late Madam Lempytzka, Miss Sophia Androsovich, was sentenced to pay a fine for contempt of court. To every question that she was asked in court she always gave one and the same reply:

"You won't believe it, but every morning when I get up I brush the hair of my soul finely, weave it into a plait and let it fall down the back... Your souls, however, are terribly tousled! But you don't notice that. No wonder, you see nothing for your tousled souls obscure your eyes... Brush your souls, gentlemen judges, jurors and you, Mr. Chief Inspector Stross!"

95

It occurred to me these days that I didn't comb through the opera in great detail concerning the death of Distelli. I *informed myself as to who now sang the role of the late Distelli in Mussorgsky's opera and went to have a cup of coffee with the famous bass, Isaac Zaborowsky.*

When asked whether it was felt in the opera that Distelli's death was solely a matter of his illness, or there were perhaps other "rumors", Zaborowsky howled with laughter, but in the midst of the laughter that seemed to suddenly age and wane in his mouth, he stiffened and rolled his eyes towards me as though he were offering me two stuffed sour kraut leaves.

"Ahem, ahem, how shall I put this... There is one information that Boris Godunoff poisoned himself. He was afraid of the whirlpool of crime and hatred that he was spreading all around him, and so he just took his heart in his hands and with a bit of stuff finished the deed..."

"A bit of what?" I asked him in astonishment.

"A bit of poison, man, what else?"

"And where did you get such information and who spreads such rumors throughout the opera?"

"What do you mean where, chief inspector? From literature, of course. When we are preparing for a part in the opera, we singers and actors inform ourselves well of its fate..."

"What fate?"

"Its life's fate."

"Are you talking about Distelli's fate or the fate of Godunoff?"

"That Boris Godunoff poisoned himself you can find in a book anonymously published in Venice as far back as 1772... It says that in our programme as well. And as far as Distelli is concerned, well he sang that role until he... shall I say, removed himself from the scene. If you

have come to ask me whether anyone here at the opera had, God forbid, removed him in any way, I assure you that there was no need at all for any such thing. Distelli finished himself off..."

And Zaborowsky shoved a programme into my hands in which it was written that the lead role in Mussorgsky's opera was now sung by him.

96

I know full well what I do not know. And this I have always known. Those matters beyond, which spiritualist deal with, remain strange to me and I am disbelieving towards that kind of world. But perhaps one should delve in such fields as well? Perhaps that is where the answer to the question of who was to blame for Lempytzka's death lies.

Having that in mind I entered a list of all my "energies" into this book - such as: hunger, pain, grief, sickness, smell, stench, joy, laughter, tears, love, thirst, etc., etc. All that which makes up the, as spiritualists say, "essence" of our life here, and the recollection of our life there, beyond death. And then I labeled those "energies" with letters from A to Z in the order in which they came to mind. There was only one thing remaining - to dream somebody else's dream, like a fortuneteller from Cairo advised me.

One morning, it seems, that really did happen to me. Somebody else woke up in my dream, it was some man, and I got up with an unfamiliar taste in my mouth and realized that I had just had somebody else's dream that faded away as soon as I looked into the first mirror. In the mirror I realized that I was "pure" and that the thought of

Lempytzka could bring about our touch. In my recollections that morning I saw Lempytzka in all her beauty, scented with the perfume "Addict Dior", and I began spying on myself to see which of my "energies" would sound up first. It was in vain, I felt nothing. Not even hunger. It wasn't until noon that I realized I had received a reply the very instant I had posed the question - smell, then. And her smell at that. Lempytzka's perfume. "Addict Dior." The appropriate letter for smell on my list of "energies" was "N". And I wrote that down in this book. So Marquezine Lempytzka had spoken up. Her reply was written out by my hand, not by dictation of Lempytzka's shade, but by dictation of the "energies" that connected us.

The letter that I wrote down the following day was "O". In my memories, however, Lempytzka was aging. She was half gray already. I was horrified. But the matter was progressing well. The letters "V", then "E", and "M" followed, and then Lempytzka fell silent. In midword. I had only "NOVEM..." written down. And then, one morning, she came into my memory somehow slim and more beautiful than ever, as though a low tide of grayness had come over her hair making it younger and younger, until finally, when I could already read the entire word, Lempytzka received her beautiful hair once more in my recollections, and those lips the color of strawberries that she used to make up reflecting herself in the eyes of Distellis' hound...

In the blue book Lempytzka's words were sending me a mysterious message with the reply to the question of who was to blame for her death. The reply was more than amazing. As though it had nothing at all to do with my question.

"NOVEMBER FIRST," *spelled out the reply.*
"Nonsense!" *was the first thing I said before I put the blue book away.*

97

After the psychiatrist at the hospital in which Distelli had died directed me towards a further search for the elements of the "family unconscious" heritage in Distelli's dream about Pushkin, according to his advice I sought out the assistance of a historian. Namely, Distelli's dream about Pushkin revolves quite considerably around violent methods ("voodoo" magic and needles) inherited from Pushkin's great-grandfather. I asked the historian recommended to me at the university whether all of that had a foundation of historical facts related to Pushkin's ancestors, or did Distelli make it all up and bring it into his dream.

As soon as he looked over Klozewitz's report on Distelli's dream, the part about Pushkin's ancestor in particular, the history professor concluded that the entire matter had a foundation of historical facts for the most part.

Realizing that I had struck against a wall once more, I listened out of politeness to the following facts about Pushkin's origin which the professor was able to inform me of:

The great-grandfather of Alexander Sergeevich Pushkin truly was from Africa, from the family of a tribal chief. He was the youngest of nineteen brothers. He had an older sister named Lagan: when he was eight years old she gave him African needles, taught him how to use them, *how to wear them hidden in his thick curly hair, she taught him how the needles could recognize him and serve him in his magic. Born and raised on the shores of the Mediterranean, they loved to bathe in the sea. The boy was grabbed there one day by slave traders. Lagan swam for a long time in vain after the ship that was carrying her brother off into the unknown world. The ship unloaded the boy at the slave market in Constantinople where he was bought by a rich aristocrat and diplomat for hire, Count Sava Vladislavich Raguzinsky. Perhaps the needles that he noticed straight away in the hair of the handsome black boy attracted the attention of the Count knowledgeable in magic who could perform witchcraft by using coins, where the age of the one the spell was to fall upon was converted into a sum of money. The new owner of the young black boy, Count Raguzinsky, was a man of power in two great states, his portrait was taken by Van Dyke, and Raguzinsky's wife was from a Venetian doge family and brought her husband a palace in Venice as dowry. His second palace Raguzinsky received in St. Petersburg from Czar Peter the Great into whose service he entered and at the Poltava battle brought something new into the art of warfare - he organized timely providing of food and ammunition to the Russian army during the battle.*

The young black boy was presented by Count Raguzinsky to the Czar who christened him in Vilna giving him his own name: Avram Petrovich Hannibal. He sent him to military schools, first Russian and then French, in Paris, and then finally married him to a bride from an upstanding Russian family. Hannibal still remained Raguzinsky's faithful friend and when the Czar sent the Count to China as his emissary, Hannibal de-

parted with him, leading the accompanying division and taking his African "voodoo" needles along, adding some Chinese needles to them upon his return. That trip with the goal to differentiate the Chinese and the Russian empires was not harmless, but Hannibal and Raguzinsky knew how to protect themselves in other ways as well, not just by means of an army..."

98

On Thursday I met with Miss Sophia Androsovich, sister of the late Lempytzka. We had tea at the "Red Rooster's" inn. It's very pleasant there, the spoons and forks are black, they served us "Aqbar" tea and African cookies made of green flour.

"Do you know what tea is?" Sophia asked me suddenly.

"?"

"What are hot beverages anyway, and our need for them? They are a replacement for blood."

"For blood?"

"Yes. For the warm blood of a freshly slaughtered animal which we have long since stopped drinking, several thousand years ago, but the thirst for it and the essential need for warm beverages, first of all milk, and when there's none to be had, for warm blood, still exists inside us. Some have not yet given up that ancient beastly need. Killers like Distelli and Lempytzka, for example. For them there was no dilemma between tea and blood..."

"I don't believe it," I told her, "there's some bloodthirsty person standing behind them who forced them to kill. I will find that somebody and then you shall see that I was right, not you."

99

"Klozewitz has been murdered!" I thought as I awoke. I dreamt somebody else's dream. They say in Egypt that other people's dreams are dreamt frequently, but cannot be memorized, and so they fade away after we awaken. As far as I know, Sophia Androsovich occasionally dreamt her sister's dreams instead of her own.

Whatever the case may be, I seem to have remembered some of that other person's dream after all. There was a stone staircase with a statue that stank of goats. Two tired mirrors were there, and somebody who sneezed as soon as he tried to laugh. I could not see him, I only saw his hand on the marble rail of the stairs. The fingers on that hand had no nails.

"Klozewitz has been murdered!" the unknown man with no fingernails told me from the darkness and sneezed once more instead of laughing.

I asked around. That other person's dream was a false alarm. Klozewitz was not murdered. Who didn't murder him?

100

Today is November first of the year 2003. I have dinner scheduled late this evening with "W", who knows more than I do about the Distelli-Cruise-Lempytzka-Hecht case. I believe that he, not Klozewitz, is behind all those murders. But his name I will not mention, not even in this diary. A house is built from the foundation, an investigation from the roof. This time I have sufficient proof to make an arrest. If I squeeze him well and if I survive the meeting I shall finally enter the name not only in this diary, but in the court annals as well.

In case I do not return from this dinner, and this remains my final note in the "blue book", the court will know whom to prosecute for my murder, for I have deposited his name in late Madam Lempytzka's safety deposit box at the "Plusquam City" bank. Only the police have had access to that deposit box since the murder of Madam Lempytzka...

P.S. Who begins his sixty-first year, and owes sixty years to the Lord, may Heaven have mercy on his soul!

The following pages are for those with their own solution to this story:

——————— ♦ ———————

Biblioteka
SAVREMENI JUGOSLOVENSKI PISCI
NA ENGLESKOM JEZIKU
Kolo 5, knjiga 4

Milorad Pavić
UNIQUE ITEM
delta novel

Za izdavača
Dijana Dereta
David Dereta

Glavni urednik
Dijana Dereta

Urednik
Jelena Pavić

Likovno grafička oprema
Marina Slavković

Distribucija samo za SCG

ISBN 86-7346-449-8

Tiraž
1000 primeraka

Beograd, 2005.

Izdavač / Štampa / Plasman
Grafički atelje *DERETA*
Vladimira Rolovića 30, 11030 Beograd
tel./faks: 011/ 25-12-221; 25-12-461
www.dereta.co.yu, office@dereta.co.yu

Knjižare *DERETA*:
Knez Mihailova 46, tel.: 011/ 30-33-503, 627-934
Banovo brdo, Dostojevskog 7, tel.: 011/30 58 707, 556-445

Milorad Pavić
UNIQUE ITEM
delta novel

For the Publisher
Dijana Dereta
David Dereta

Editor-in-Chief
Dijana Dereta

Editor
Jelena Pavić

Artistic and Graphic Design
Marina Slavković

Distribution for SCG only

ISBN 86-7346-449-8

Number of copies printed
1000

Belgrade, 2005.

Published / Printed / Placement

Grafički atelje *DERETA*
Vladimira Rolovića 30, 11030 Belgrade
phone/fax: +381 11 25 12 221; +381 11 25 12 461
www.dereta.co.yu, office@dereta.co.yu

Bookstore *DERETA*
Knez Mihailova 46, phone: +381 11 30 33 503,
+381 11 62 79 34
Banovo brdo, Dostojevskog 7
phone: +381 11 30 58 707, +381 11 55 64 45

CIP - Каталогизација у публикацији
Народна библиотека Србије, Београд

821.163.41-31

PAVIĆ, Milorad
 Unique Item : delta novel with a hundred endings / Milorad Pavić ; translated by Dragana Rajkov. - 1st English Ed. - Belgrade : Dereta, 2005 (Belgrade : Dereta). - 250 str. ; 21 cm. - (Biblioteka Savremeni jugoslovenski pisci na engleskom jeziku ; kolo 5, knj. 4)

Prevod dela: Unikat. - Tiraž 1.000.

ISBN 86-7346-449-8

COBISS.SR-ID 120146444